SISTERS OF THE
VAST BLACK

LINA RATHER

A TOM DOHERTY ASSOCIATES BOOK

NEW YORK

This is a work of fiction. All of the characters, organizations, and events portrayed in this novella are either products of the author's imagination or are used fictitiously.

SISTERS OF THE VAST BLACK

Cover art and design by Drive Communications

Edited by Christie Yant

A Tor.com Book
Published by Tom Doherty Associates
120 Broadway
New York, NY 10271

www.tor.com

Tor® is a registered trademark of

Macmillan Publishing Group, LLC.

ISBN 978-1-250-26026-0 (ebook)
ISBN 978-1-250-26025-3 (trade paperback)

First Edition: October 2019

I.

Orate Fratres

WHILE THE SISTERS OF THE *Our Lady of Impossible Constellations* argued themselves in circles, the Reverend Mother sat silently in her chair at the head of the chapel as she always did, listening to the arguments twist and double back on themselves.

Sister Lucia argued that the ship, being a beast and therefore not in possession of a rational soul, did not have a responsibility to follow the dictates of their order. Sister Varvara countered that convents were sacred places. The ship, be it beast or plant or mineral, had been consecrated according to doctrine. Allowing it to continue on its present course was a clear desecration and would be a blemish on all their souls. Sister Varvara had a face like the surface of an uninhabited moon, gray and stern. Usually, that face of hers brooked no argument.

They were burning too many precious chemlights on this debate. While Sister Ewostatewos delivered a long soliloquy on the early Church's treatment of barnyard animals and how that might possibly illuminate their current dilemma regarding the ship, the Reverend Mother looked up to the spot where the crucifix hung. Every shipbound convent and poor colony ministry had the same one, mass-produced on Old Earth and brought by the crateful by newly ordained priests doing their hardship posts out here in the black. The Reverend Mother hung this one on the wall herself forty years ago, right after the end of the war, when she was a young woman and the ship was newly consecrated. They'd both been so young then. After she had affixed the crucifix to the ship's inner membrane with a dab of bioglue under each of the nails, she had laid her head against the muculent wall and listened to the heartbeat pumping fluid across the ship's undulating body.

It had been a long time since Old Earth sent shipfuls of young priests out into the dark with identical crucifixes to convert the prodigal colonies. The Reverend Mother's crucifix was a relic of a different age, an age of order and conformity.

"Mother," Sister Gemma said, drawing her back from her reverie. "I'm afraid we're no closer to a consensus."

The Reverend Mother shook her head at her crucifix. She and the small Lord, they shared an understanding. She raised her hands.

Sister Lucia came forward and knelt by her side to

watch her hands move. Most of them understood some signing, but she was the best at it.

"We shall think upon this matter for three days," Sister Lucia translated. "And reconvene."

"What about our bishop?" Sister Mary Catherine asked. She was stout and squat and the only one of the sisters to be Earth-born, and secretly in their sinful hearts the others believed this had warped her to be too reliant on hierarchical authority. They ignored her. Any communication with Earth would take three weeks to arrive from these outer reaches and another three weeks for the bishop to convey his opinion back. By that time, their decision would have been made one way or the other.

Thankfully, only Sister Lucia knew her well enough to see the small catches in her signing. Irritation, tiredness. Sister Mary Catherine was a new aspirant, directed to their convent because she wanted to minister to the godless outer systems. Apparently no one on Earth had told her that the farther systems had plenty of gods, or that the sisters of the *Our Lady of Impossible Constellations* spent more time tending wounds of the flesh than bringing heathens to Christ and preferred it that way. She likely was not long for their company.

"The Reverend Mother says she shall send a message to the Vatican tonight."

And she would, even though there was much to be

done. They had been called to a new colony in need of marriages and a baptism, and they would make landfall on that moon in just a few hours. They had been indulging themselves too long in this. "Until then, let us prepare ourselves for the approach to Phoyongsa III. We shall fast from the next bell until landfall."

Sister Mary Catherine opened her mouth again, but Sister Faustina cut her off so smoothly it seemed like an accident. "As you say, Mother."

The Reverend Mother clapped her hands together, and the quorum was dispersed. There was work to be done. Always work, even on a pulmonate-ship like this that didn't require oiling or welding or spare parts. Sister Mary Catherine and Sister Ewostatewos were on plant duty, so that they could all continue to eat. Sister Gemma's duty was caring for the ship itself as it bore them through the stars. Most of the others went to rest or meditation. And Sister Faustina would monitor the communication array. The Lord worked in mysterious ways and strange places, here in the eternal dark. A call could come at any time and so someone always kept vigil.

The Reverend Mother was left alone in the chapel. She stretched out her hands and tried to stop them shaking. She was old but the tremble in her hands belonged to someone older still. She'd managed to cover it so far.

As she left, she laid her hand on the hatch between this

room and the control bay. Beneath this stretch of damp skin ran one of the ship's two main blood vessels and she could feel the pressure of the hemolymph pumping from the heart, through the invertebrate musculature, past digestive tubules and branching nerve clusters, forward to the head. She offered up a quick prayer for the heart, that it may continue to pump and sustain them all.

$\sim$

Sister Gemma went to her laboratory. She had set a diagnostic panel up to run through the quorum, and the results would be in by now. She wanted a solution, though she knew there was no clean one.

Before she could check the results, the ship needed tending.

She mixed a hormone injection by dropper and tested it by rubbing a droplet on a patch of ship-flesh she had cultured in a petri dish. The flesh flushed a healthy celadon. The ship was good at taking care of itself, but ten human lives still strained it. The injections sped along waste processing and absorption of excess protein and methane. She prepared a syringe and tapped it to release the air bubbles inside. To her knowledge no one had ever discovered what happened when a living ship had an embolism; she did not intend on being the one to find out.

Before she took vows, Sister Gemma had grown up on a shipyard in orbit around Saturn. Her first job, at four-teen and a half, was coaxing juvenile ships from their lar-val stage—where they looked like any *Elysia chlorotica* clinging to any coast on Old Earth—to the stage where they could be introduced to the vacuum. In shipyards, captive ships were bred by hand by biologists. Each in-dividual's genome was sequenced and mates chosen ac-cording to size estimates and risk of genetic disease. Ship-wrights waited by the grand mating-ships until they re-leased gelatinous ribbons of eggs like knobbly seaweed. The eggs were too fragile to stay in the airless dark, and so the shipwrights attached them to lattices in climate-controlled bays and culled the eggs down as they grew. A batch of thousands of eggs might produce only five or six viable ships, and only one or two of those would be sizable enough to house more than a dozen crew. It was a process about as far from God as it was possible to be. But there in that bay, spreading nutrient-slush across the lattices, Sister Gemma had her first glimpse of the divine in the slugs' splitting cells and symbiotic photosynthesis.

Now she used a scalpel to cut through the mucus membrane that protected the ship's inner flesh from ir-ritants. She touched the tip of the needle to the pulsing viridian muscle and it quivered under her touch. A ship's muscle tissue was soft and translucent, just strong enough to stand up to the pressures of space.

Behind her, the hatch made a soft sucking noise. Sister Ewostatewos pulled herself through, carrying a basket. She riffled through the cabinets of chemical additives, searching for something.

"What's wrong?" Sister Gemma asked.

"A slight iron deficiency in the beds. Nothing unexpected. We haven't taken on unfiltered water recently." Sister Ewostatewos poured a packet of soil supplement into a vial of a clear liquid and shook it. This she'd attach to the hydroponics bay's feeder line and let it flow into the soybeans and carrots they'd planted last week. "You're hesitating."

Sister Gemma let the syringe drop and pressed her gloved hand against the naked muscle to keep the membrane from knitting itself back together. "Yes."

Sister Ewostatewos was the newest of them, besides Sister Mary Catherine, who barely counted since they all knew they weren't keeping her. She'd grown up on an airless moon, in a bubble. Her father was an Ethiopian Orthodox and her mother a Catholic, which she intimated was a strange partnership. Lately, Sister Gemma had wanted to ask her how she had come to pick one over the other, but some things were too private to ask after. Or too difficult to explain.

"I'm worried it's my fault," she said.

"The ship preparing for mating?"

"Yes." Sister Gemma swallowed. The muscle twitched under her hand: small electrical impulses spasming in the nerves to remind her where she was. "I am responsible for its care. It's so young for mating. Most ships don't mature for another twenty or thirty years. Perhaps I wasn't regulating its hormones correctly. Or I missed a vitamin deficiency."

"Is that possible?"

Sister Gemma shrugged. Many things were possible. Almost anything. They lived at the very outer bounds of what was known. Back on Old Earth people studied living ships in laboratories and moon-based testing facilities with limitless budgets for breeding programs and genetic studies. They raised generation after generation of ships under endless variables. And even there, no one could be sure what caused one neonate to develop into a viable ship and another to mature to be chamberless and unusable. When she first noticed the ship's changing hormonal profile, and its odd behavior, she had thought it was the early signs of organ failure. Then she discovered that the ship had imprinted on a mate somewhere in their voyage and was trying to follow its pheromone trail to fulfill their biological imperative. This was a relief for the two seconds before she began to think about the theological implications. "I sent a message to two of the leading research shipyards. But a response won't arrive in time."

"If you did the best you could, then everything else was up to God."

Sister Ewostatewos only said such things when they were true, which made her one of Sister Gemma's favorite people. In this life there were many people whose mouths were full of empty platitudes.

"I'm afraid," Sister Gemma confessed. Of more than the ship, though she couldn't say that.

"There will always be difficult choices. And even if we are the first religious house to face this dilemma, we won't be the last. More and more orders are taking to living ships every year. Perhaps we will be remembered in teachings for it. How many of us will be remembered at all?"

"How prideful of you."

Sister Ewostatewos laughed at the joke it was. "We're all only human. Cheer up, sister. None of us can change what was."

"You're right of course." Sister Gemma pulled her hand away from the ship's muscle and pressed the syringe smoothly into it. The muscle twitched and then relaxed and she depressed the plunger. The edges of the membrane had gone dry and tacky because of her dallying. She rubbed a dab of moisturizing gel over them. The ship didn't even need her to press them together—as soon as the gel had absorbed the incision disappeared seamlessly. She would never, never cease to be amazed by these ships. Even if she left shiplife forever one day, she would never forget the feel of its heartbeat surrounding her.

"I didn't hear your vote earlier. May I ask?"

"I haven't come to a decision. I don't believe the ship has a soul, or a holy obligation. If we owned a cow, we would allow it to reproduce. And yet, we don't live inside a cow. Livestock is not consecrated." Sister Gemma shook her head. "Every argument I think of, I can counter."

"Maybe you'll come to an answer when we turn the gravity off. I find it clears my head."

"Perhaps."

Sister Ewostatewos smiled at her and took her mineral supplements back through the hatch. When she was gone, Sister Gemma touched the spot she had just sliced open, now as smooth as a newborn calf's wet skin. She didn't believe the ship had a soul. But she did believe it could want. Maybe if she stayed here, listening, she would hear its voice. Maybe it would tell her what to do.

～

Sister Faustina made herself a cup of tea with plenty of cream and sugar. This was not, perhaps, in keeping with the spirit of the upcoming fast, but she would drink it down before the next bell. They weren't Poor Clares, after all, set on depriving themselves of every earthly comfort. No sense in depriving yourself now when there was plenty of deprivation yet to come. When the water boiled she picked a packet of green tea from the drawer and stirred it until the powder dissolved. She had heard that tea—real tea—was a kind of plant leaf, but she had never seen such a thing. It sounded just like the kind of resource-intensive wastefulness that Old Earthers were fond of. She allowed herself two scoops each from the cream and sugar canisters and let them turn her tea a pale brown like parcel paper.

She screwed the top onto her cup and settled herself into her chair in front of the communications array. Whoever had first grown this ship had been a lot taller, and the chair was never quite comfortable, no matter how many times she asked Sister Gemma to please readjust it. Ships always kept an imprint of their original design, and this one refused to grow a headrest three inches lower on the lump of fat that was her chair.

She set her cup to the left of the screen and rubbed her thumb over the soft moss covering the console until it grew up the sides of the cup to hold it in place. First she had to review the petitioning colony's data. It was rare, but some convents were lured to their deaths with fake prayer requests. Ships were valuable, as were all their other supplies. The farther you got from Earth, the harder it was to find chemlights or processed chromium or medicine made by someone with a university degree.

Sister Faustina opened the colony's message. First—a burst of advertisements. *Best food in the third system! Repair your vessel at Vishni and Sons—we specialize in liveship propulsion repair! Come settle our beautiful moon—you've never seen water as clear as this!* All sorts of signals piggybacked off of legitimate communications. Below the advertisements, older signals rolled over each other in the background audio. Some even prewar. Propagandist broadcasts and audiodramas, most read by Mrs. August, the never-named voice of Earth Central Governance. She'd done years and years of broadcasts, all in that particular, beautiful voice of hers. Even after the war, when she'd very likely died in one of the bombings, outer-system children had grown up listening to her bedtime stories, because it didn't cost coin for the download rights.

Sister Faustina made a note to update their spam filter next time they docked at a station with a half-decent programmer.

The colony had sent a video, which was really an unwarranted expense, but did make it easier to verify their identities. Five people crowded into the screen.

"We send our greetings to the sisters of the *Our Lady of Impossible Constellations,*" the woman in the center said. She spoke Earth English carefully. Her accent was familiar—Sister Faustina had also grown up speaking the patois of the asteroids and shipwreck belts. She knew exactly where this woman was from, with her tightly coiled dark hair and thin eyes and soft sienna skin. And from the real tell—her inherited heterochromia. The Plutonian Archipelago. A junkyard of ships left to wreck at the very edge of the first system. The Archipelago had been settled by two families, one Nigerian and one Tibetan, who built a salvage empire in a worthless trash heap. The Phuntsok family was legendary. For generations they had been the kings of scavenge. Most of them had also been killed in the war when they stood against Earth. As far as Sister Faustina knew, the Archipelago was just a shimmering band of debris around the cold planetoid's gravity well now. This young woman was probably the second generation to grow up outside it. "We are establishing a new colony on the moon Phoyongsa III. We would like our moon blessed, and three couples would like to be married. And—" She smiled. The darker-skinned man beside her had to be her husband, the way he beamed. "—we will have a baby to be baptized by then. We are sending the coordinates of our moon. We have supplies to trade as well. We eagerly await your reply."

Sister Faustina checked their colony register and inventory list and found all in order. A baptism was always fun. There would be alcohol of some sort to go around—barley wine, probably—and the baby would be passed hand to hand, there would be real fire and soil-grown food.

There was another message in the bank, also directed specifically to them. How unusual. It had come a long, long way. Based on its signature and the trail of satellites and ships and breaches it had traveled through, it was from the first system.

Sister Faustina sipped her tea. A message from the first system was either very good or very bad. For the forty years since the Great War, Old Earth had retreated inward and left the other three systems mostly to their own affairs. Lately, the gray lady seemed to be stirring. Sister Faustina had seen more and more traders sponsored by Earth Central Governance taking the jumps to the second, third, and fourth systems, bringing with them tantalizing things that only Earth could produce, like silk and real black pepper and prewar wine and that wet-leaf tea they deified. It looked to Sister Faustina an awful lot like they wanted to bring their children back under their iron fist.

The message was sealed with their cardinal's encryption. She entered the key. Only two people on the ship knew it, herself and the Mother Superior. They heard from the cardinal so rarely that it took her two tries. Usually these messages were about changes in protocol—the desired length of wimple for their order, a new translation of the liturgies, what station had a shipment of communion wafers available. They had not seen a priest in three years. It was hardly necessary. A century ago the Fourth Vatican Council had allowed sisters of the religious life to perform every sacrament but confession, confirmation, and ordination. There weren't enough priests out in the black to do it. And anyway, that was how it had been in the beginning.

Dearest sisters of the Our Lady of Impossible Constellations, the message began, *His Holiness Pius XVI, Bishop of Rome, Vicar of Jesus Christ, Successor of the Prince of the Apostles, Supreme Pontiff of the Universal Church, Primate of Italy, Archbishop and Metropolitan of the Roman Province, Sovereign of the Vatican City State, Servant of the servants of God, has decreed that there will be an accounting of the officiants of the Church.*

The last she'd heard, the Pope was Urban X, and he was dead. The announcement of Pius XVI's appointment must have gotten lost. She did not like the sound of "an accounting," but then, Sister Faustina was often told she had too great a mistrust of authority.

A priest will meet you at your next convenient docking. He shall take an accounting of your numbers and activities and send it back to the Holy See. The assigned priest will be overseeing three convents, including yours, and split his time between them accordingly.

Sister Faustina groped for her tea and swallowed two mouthfuls fast enough to burn the inside of her throat all the way down.

His Holiness has decreed this as part of the continuing efforts to repair the Church after the Great War, and to minister to as many souls as possible. Further instruction will be sent.—Card. R. Capul.

"Then why don't you put the priest on his own ship?" she muttered. The message was dated two months ago. Further instruction had almost certainly already been provided, and was waiting in a relay station somewhere for them to get in range of the signal.

She resealed the message so no one without the key could read it. No one would. She trusted most of her sisters, and the ones that she didn't trust were not the kind for subterfuge.

Some of the other orders would welcome a return to the days of hierarchy. Not many of the shipbound ones. But she could imagine some planetary sisters longing for a past of rules and authority. You didn't have to be so flexible when you had an atmosphere to hold you close and let you breathe all the air you could ever want.

The hatch behind her opened. Sister Faustina knew it was the Mother Superior by her creaking bones.

"Is the colony confirmed?" she signed. "Any other news?"

Sister Faustina considered the message. There were no secrets in convents, they said. But there were secrets wherever there were humans to have them. "Phoyongsa III checks out. Other than that—just spam."

The Mother Superior was staring at Sister Faustina's screen. Sister Faustina looked back, but she hadn't forgotten to hide the cardinal's message.

"Mother?"

The older woman squinted at her and then, slowly, nodded. "Very good."

"Perhaps you should sleep a bit, before we land."

Any of the other sisters, even Mary Catherine, would have had more luck. The Reverend Mother barely managed an indulgent smile for Sister Faustina's meddling. "Always work to be done, Sister."

The Reverend Mother smacked the button next to the hatch, and the contracted muscle relaxed when the electrical current running through it changed. She stepped through and was gone. The current changed back, the muscle contracted, and the hatch sealed back up with a damp pop. Sister Faustina reopened the cardinal's message and read it again. She would show it to the Reverend

Mother. Just not yet. She needed to think over it first. It was an ugly portent to have the Church decide it wanted to be a central dictate again. She had grown up in the ruins of the last war and had no desire to see another. Even if they would have to bring Venus and Mars and the Saturn moon colonies under their iron fist before they reached out for the second and third systems.

And right after the ascension of a new pope. She didn't know anything about this new one, but she had kept her ear to the ground. New nuns and priests who had been educated in the first system called Earth *His chosen cradle.* They spoke about a future under Central Governance like a good thing, with the thoughtless repetition of children who hadn't yet learned to question what their teachers said. Orders who spent most of their time in the second system, just one jump away from Earth, said new rules were coming faster than they had in a generation. Little things—what cloth was appropriate for women of the religious life, what questions should be asked of a marrying couple before the marriage would be performed, the order of hymns. All starting in the last few years, when the old pope had taken to his sickbed.

And there were whispers among the new colonists coming here to the third system. Central Governance attempting to collect on old, prewar land claims in the Mars Republic and the Saturn polities. Fresh-eyed young

Earthlings arriving on new colonies armed with gifts of expensive agricultural tech and leaflets espousing the glorious benevolence of Central Governance.

Sister Faustina had listened to all these reports with growing horror. It sounded like Central Governance wanted another war. It sounded like they had forgotten the death, the irradiated lifeless colonies that would lay fallow for generations, the plagues of swallowpox and that beast ringeye leaving towns full of nothing but corpses, the shipfuls of frozen bleeding bodies that still drifted derelict all across the systems.

Her mothers and father had been soldiers in that war, and after ECG had abandoned them when the supply chains failed, they indentured themselves to a mining moon and died one after the other of redlung, hacking up bits of themselves with every wracking cough. The air on that moon went out so often that Sister Faustina had learned spacesign before she was out of diapers. The stories said that the language only required one hand so that you could cling to a safety rail with the other and save yourself from the vacuum. Secretly she thought it was because so many people lost limbs on the small hardscrabble colonies.

When she was sixteen, burying her father, she realized she was too poor for the customary pyres, too poor for passage away, too poor to buy herself any life but the dust-choked one that had killed her parents. And so she had gone to the only church on the moon and claimed that her heart was full of God and begged the priest to sponsor her as a novice.

She was religious enough, yes—in the way that everyone who stepped foot outside of gravity's embrace was religious. They all prayed in the dark, be it to the Christian God or the Islamic one or the Hindu many-faced pantheon or the cruel, calculating, exacting god of Science.

The Reverend Mother knew the truth, of course. They had an understanding. She had accepted Sister Faustina in her novitiate, and on the eve of her vows, called her to a private audience.

"Why did you choose this path?" the Reverend Mother had signed.

Sister Faustina looked into the Mother Superior's eyes and knew there was no point in lying. "I want to be of service. And I want to see this universe that I am but a speck in."

"You do not feel called to glorify Him and His works?"

"I want to do good." It was true. Even in her short novitiate she had seen enough dying men brought peace by the ritual of a sacrament to believe that this was a good life to lead. "I do not think I am filled with His light as others are. I see this as—a match for my talents."

"You will not have a family of your own body. You cannot break your vows for the pleasures of the flesh. I will have you expelled if you do."

"I have never felt drawn to such pleasures, Mother."

"You will not marry anyone, or officiate funerals, or baptize. Those are sacred duties and I will not have them cheapened."

"Words are not my talent anyway." She knew machines and their intricacies, and she knew logistics and careful planning. Her tongue had always been clumsy and graceless.

"Very well," the Reverend Mother had said. This was space and to survive, the old ways must be bent. They had never spoken of her shaky faith again.

For sixteen years, Sister Faustina had served aboard the *Our Lady of Impossible Constellations*. She had held cool cloths to the foreheads of plague victims and she had learned the basics of surgery. She had gathered up orphaned children and heard the last words of the dying. She cared for the communications array, and the machinery in the hydroponics bay, and all the other metal appendages grafted onto the beast that ferried them through the stars. More times than she could count she had put on a suit and stickboots and clambered outside to reposition antennae or rewrap wiring into the folds of the ship's skin (like rubber, it was, like the soles of good strong work boots that would keep a man in a hard job alive). She rarely prayed outside of collective worship, but out there, when she was separated from the heavens by only a few millimeters of alloy and glass, she felt God blazing from every planet and star.

She would give her life for this ship. She would do whatever it took to protect this small life she had built. And that was why she did not tell the Reverend Mother about the message.

There were other matters to attend to anyway—the communications log recorded three outgoing messages. One was from Sister Lucia to the university on Taurus IX, asking for yet another article to be sent. Two were from Sister Gemma. The first was an accounting of their current predicament with the ship's desire to mate and a long report on its physiology, sent to a shipwright in the second system. The second she had tried to cover with a boring subject line, but Sister Faustina recognized the recipient. She had been following Sister Gemma's correspondence.

Yet another secret she was keeping that the Reverend Mother should have known about. But she believed in letting people make their decisions in private. And more than that: she did not like how the Reverend Mother was changing this past year.

~

After twelve bells of quiet travel, they arrived at Phoyongsa III in what was morning on that moon. The whole ship shivered when they broke the atmosphere. Outside, it was unfurling its tough outer skin to reveal the soft, darker-green flesh underneath and absorb the filtered sunlight. It would expand its cilia to drink in the moisture from the clouds and all of the nutrients—helium, mostly, on this little ball of rock—that it could not take in when it was compacted against the pressures of space. The sisters pressed their faces against the portholes to feel real sunlight, even though the radiation didn't penetrate the glass. This sun was a swollen old giant hanging red-orange and huge over the horizon. Below, orange tarps marked where soon there would be houses and a communal kitchen and a mine shaft or a trade post or whatever these ones had decided to take on for their industry.

When they set down, Sister Faustina helped Sister Varvara heave the gangplank down from the wall. Once they'd set it down on the lip of one of the ship's calloused plates, she shaded her eyes to look out over the colony.

The earth was red here, iron-rich, good for crops like sweet potatoes and radishes. The colonists were already working on the sweet potatoes. The thin green stems had been carefully planted in rows of moist brown mounds on the eastern side of the settlement. Rabbits sat fattening in a pen, chickens in another. From the gangplank, the rabbits looked like Mars variants. Very fine hair, very pale. Someday, if this colony lasted long enough and did not add to the gene pool too often, there would be a Phoyongsa III subspecies. Or maybe the colony would not last, but the rabbits would survive, and they would grow and mate and feed alone for generations, until they were no longer a subspecies at all.

The sisters crowded the open hatch. After months in the ship and orbital stations, the sunlight tingled. The air smelled of so many layered things—flowers, dung, livestock, and cool breeze off water. Sister Lucia helped the Reverend Mother down from the gangplank first.

"Welcome." The captain greeted them first. Her name was Terret, a Venusian name, taken from the bright blue birds that flourished on the floating habitats there. She carried a baby with the big, dark eyes of the man beside her. The other colonists huddled behind them, maybe thirty in all. They had already set a long table down the middle of their only road. Sister Faustina picked out the engaged couples by the way they held each other's hands so gingerly, as if the sisters might actually deny them a ceremony. "Please come and share a meal with us. It's not much, I'm afraid, but . . ."

"I'm sure it's lovely," Sister Faustina replied.

Terret nodded and hurried to the table. They were all so nervous. Even the ones of other religions—and

Faustina picked out a couple of Hindus and a Buddhist on first sweep. So much could go wrong in a new colony. Ecosystems were so fragile, and humans were such a strain. One wrong step and they could turn their paradise into a desolate rock.

This was part of why their order still wore the old style black robes, wimples, and habits. For a long, long time, they had done away with such vestments. It made sense when they were confined to Earth. Here, out where there had never been a government truly (and there certainly wasn't one anymore) the vestments made them stand out. They were a passport through war zones and onto stations whose docking charges they would not have otherwise been able to afford. And in situations like this, a new colony fresh off the ship, they were a bit of a good luck charm.

This colony was so fresh that their deadship was only half broken-down. One thruster lay against the poly-clad exterior of the back of the ship, and a pile of titanium doors lay stacked on the ground. Soon enough the colonists would have those broken down to component pieces or put through a recycler for the raw metal, and then they would go to building houses or tillers or furnaces.

There was no church here, but they didn't need one. A bowl of water would do for the baby, a few tall grasses lashed together in the half-shell of a house would be enough of an arch for the marriages. Sister Ewostatewos had the communion wafers and the licenses that they would transmit to the authorities who mattered in this system. Another copy would be attached to the colony-grant. Sister Gemma had taken the crucifix down from the chapel and was already clambering up on top of crates of rice and seeds to put it up on the wall of a roof-less house.

"Please," Terret said. They had spread two tables in the middle of the town, already laden with rice and stewed beef tack. "I'm starving. Everything I eat the little one takes, I swear."

"Babies will do that," Sister Varvara said. "May I hold him?" And with that, the tension broke and they all sat down to eat.

The food was simple. Mostly leftover rations. Dried beef stewed with tomato paste and spices and water into a mouth-tingling curry. Rice cooked with dried lime leaves. A salad made from a flat moss that grew here that was crunchy like butter lettuce with the flavor of leeks, dressed in vinegar and mustard. For dessert, brown sugar cooked in powdered milk and agar agar until it became a caramel pudding. The fresh meat—on this moon, that consisted of lizards long as a forearm, six of them sitting in a pen—would wait for the wedding. It was delicious, all of it.

Sister Faustina scraped up rice with the side of her spoon along with a long trail of curry that had collected in the rim of her plate. The plates were Martian china—she could tell by the pattern, a mountain-range design that had been popular before the war—and heavy. It would have cost a lot to bring them here in fuel and lost cargo space. "These are lovely."

"Thank you," Terret said. She pointed to her husband, a tall and quiet man. "They are from Joseph's family. They were a wedding present, an heirloom. We were living off gov-issue fiber-pulp plates before."

Another man scooped more rice into another pot set over a burning fuel canister. The canvas bag was marked with the nine-planet stylization of the first system and CENTRAL GOVERNANCE ISSUED over the date stamp.

"Did you spend time on Earth?" Sister Faustina asked. A polite way around to her real questions.

Terret shook her head. "They have stations around the first system where you can go and get your vaccines and supplies. They've got a whole charitable arm for small colony-shares like us—the New Worlds Foundation. I wouldn't have done it if not for the price—my parents still hate Central Governance, even though the old government's nothing but a memory and a couple of blast sites back on Earth now. But it was so cheap. The whole package—standard ration pack, vaccines and med kits, chemlights and fuel canisters—was half of what we'd have paid on an independent station. All we had to do was sit through a presentation and take some pamphlets, and we recycled the pamphlets as soon as we left orbit. They made us promise to send them statistical data, but it wasn't anything we wouldn't be broadcasting anyhow."

Joseph sighed into his plate.

"You didn't like the deal?" Sister Faustina asked. Sister Lucia frowned at her from across the table. This was supposed to be a happy day, and she was spoiling it with questions. Oh, well. She would stop before she ruined any matrimonial harmony.

"Not so long ago they were bombing us," Joseph said. "And now, we take their propaganda."

"We didn't listen to it," Terret argued. "What's the harm in wasting their paper?"

"I think they forget their defeat too quickly," Joseph said, and picked his spoon back up to put an end to the matter.

"It's a good thing we didn't have Keret yet." Terret hugged the boy close to her. She must be very capable, to juggle being a captain and the leader of a colony and a mother. Any one of those was a full-time job. "He would have hated the vaccines. We gave him the after-birth ones and he wailed like he was being born again."

One of the other colonists rolled up her sleeve. She had a dark-red spot on her upper arm, a cluster of three pinpricks. "Hurt like anything, I'll tell you."

Sister Lucia leaned over her plate to peer at the mark. "That's a war-issue multi-syringe. It lets you inject a whole batch of immunizations at once, for expediency. Usually more than just the three-or five-set you'd be getting for a new colony. They're certainly not throwing much money behind this propagandist venture."

"The war took its toll." Terret's face darkened and Sister Faustina wondered if she was thinking about the famous Phuntsok dynasty, just a memory now, the family scattered across the four systems and scattering further with each baby born under an unfamiliar sky. "Maybe they don't have the capital."

The mood had grown somber. Pressed fiber cutlery scraped against heirloom plates with all the noise of a grasshopper leaping from one stalk of grass to another. The baby slept fitfully, his small hands balled into angry fists. One of the colonists—a young man with a headful of painstaking braids—lifted his fork toward the Mother Superior. "Reverend Mother, you must have seen the war. Tell us, what was it like, to live it? My grandparents would never speak of it, and we were only from the second system."

The Reverend Mother was focused on her plate, mixing her curry into her rice carefully and methodically so each grain was covered the same. She ate less these days, Sister Faustina had noticed. One more thing that was none of her business. Let the old woman wither if she wanted. And yet, the way she scooped the rice up and over, over and over, it was unsettling. When the young man spoke, she didn't put down the spoon, just watched him for a long, quiet moment.

A quick sign, her left hand. "The war?"

"Yes, Mother. I just wondered . . ." He fell silent.

"The war was hell."

The colonists looked at each other, then back down at their plates. No one ate.

"The Reverend Mother does not like to speak much of those times," Sister Lucia said. She reached out, like she wanted to put a hand on the Reverend Mother's shoulder, and then remembered how inappropriate that would be. The Reverend Mother held her hand up, flat-palmed, to stop her.

"I mean biblically," she signed. "It was hell. The land was turned to churning fire and ash. Sulfur choked a continent dead. I saw California slide into the ocean, I was close enough to watch the line of bombs go off across the fault line one by one, each as visible as a city at night from that distance. You cannot imagine a thing like that, child. Millions dead before they could call for help. A cloud of dust covering a hemisphere."

"You were in orbit for the end?" Sister Lucia asked. "I thought . . . I suppose I assumed . . . that you were much farther out in the first system when it all ended."

The Reverend Mother's hands fell into her lap, still and silent. She stared at her food, and for a moment Sister Faustina thought the old woman had gone and fallen asleep there at the table. But no, she lifted her right hand.

"I was close enough. I'm sorry—this is a very difficult topic. Please excuse me if I do not go on." Her hand shook. She had never seemed frail before—old, of course, in the way that a towering tree was old—but not frail. Now she did.

The rest of the dinner party looked at each other over the table.

"No, excuse me," the young man said. "I have a little fascination with it, that's all. This is supposed to be a happy evening. I'm sorry for bringing it up."

Joseph stood up from the table. "I have just the thing!"

He ducked into the half-disassembled ship and rattled around in the stack of crates waiting to be unboxed. He returned with a brown bottle wrapped in a cream-colored handwritten label.

"This is honey wine from my grandmother's bees, stored in her cellar, given to me by my mother to bless our new home with." He split the wax from the top and dislodged the cork with a practiced twist. They had only thin plastic cups, but the wine poured golden like the best summer sunset, and around the tables shoulders relaxed again. "Don't worry—she gave me enough to bless us thrice over. Plenty left to get properly drunk at the weddings."

Sister Faustina swallowed a mouthful and it went down warm and sweet and still cool from inside the crate. The moon was just spinning into springtime, but the wine warmed her straight through from her tongue to her fingertips. She swallowed another mouthful and this time the honey came to the fore, sugar and muskiness coating the inside of her mouth. She had tasted real wine only rarely, and had never understood the words in the old cookbooks and romantic novels that came across the relays. Oakey or dry or soil-tasting. This was sweet, then warm, then bitter in the back of her mouth, gently encouraging her to take another sip for the sweetness.

Joseph lifted the bottle to the light and there, in the bottom, was a preserved honeybee. A real one, its wings scattering the light through the glass.

~

That night they slept with the hatch open and the wind whistling through the ship. The moss that covered the walls rippled in its wake, like waves, like the ship reaching out toward atmosphere. They needed no chemlights—the glow of the planet above and the unclouded stars left the night a soft blue, bright enough to see by, or write by. Sister Lucia couldn't sleep, so she slipped from her chamber to sit in the grass beside the ship with paper and a sharpened pencil.

For her daily meditation she was working on a biography of Saint Adetayo, who had spent her life growing the first living ship and who had through her devotion allowed humanity to spread across the stars without needing to suck dry the Earth. She had just reached the part where Adetayo, stripped of funding by her university and with only trays of greenless veliger-stage neonates to show for her efforts, was on the verge of losing her faith. There was not much more to go—much of the saint's later life had been lost to the inevitable ravages of history.

Once she finished writing the hagiography by hand, Sister Lucia would record it and set the recording into a satellite that they would launch into solar orbit so that the story of Saint Adetayo would broadcast indefinitely to be heard and shared by all who encountered the signal. Sister Lucia knew hubris was a sin, but she swelled with pride when she imagined her words living long beyond her mortal body, the signal traveling farther and farther to alien worlds not yet dreamed of by human imaginations. Someday humanity's language would be strange, stranger even than the patois spoken in the farthest systems now, but the words would persist.

She had taken on hagiography because there were long stretches where they were alone with little need for doctoring. Usually it brought her clarity. Today she found herself unable to untangle the threads of the saint's life. Saint Adetayo had left no journals. None of her private words were extant, lost between the plague at the end of the saint's century, and the rebellions after, and then the war only a generation ago. Sister Lucia was at the pivotal moment—the loss of faith, the moment when all might have been undone. Some creative interpretation was necessary to evoke the despair, the burning desire for progress that led Saint Adetayo to press on.

When she was a child, the only teacher on the asteroid had told Sister Lucia she loved too many things too deeply. She loved the rovers that rumbled her lullabies and the little spider-legged bots that rattled overhead repairing microfissures in the glass dome that kept them alive. She loved the roly-poly bugs that aerated the soil in the gardens and the aphids that cleaned the plants. She loved her parents and the other children and that teacher despite his lack of love for anything that wasn't a person. Later when she took her aptitude tests and began her medical training, she learned to love skin and bone and microbiomes and mitochondria, the miraculous architecture of humanity. What a glorious universe, to have made beings so complicated and fragile! She loved them all, each and every one. When she took her vows, she had seen the great history of them stretching behind her, all of her dead sisters who linked hands and brought her here, to this one moment, which could not have been any other way.

She wrote, *Alone in her darkened laboratory, Saint Adetayo sat with her trays of failed ships, contemplating their small lives. Each one a failure, a chance for humanity to see the stars realized and then extinguished by the unyielding rules of genetics. She had no one left beside her. This was a fool's errand, a project for a crackpot scientist who had lost sight of the laws of nature, according to her department chair. Saint Adetayo had only righteousness left, and the knowledge that she had a gift for humanity that would change the entire course of history and take them from their small and dying planet to a great wide universe.*

She took the blunt side of her pencil and drew a dark black line through all of it.

Certainty? Is that what the saint had felt? Certainty? How could she have felt certainty in anything? How could she have known that she was on the cusp of a miracle and not instead meddling in God's design?

Sister Lucia tried again. *Alone in her darkened laboratory, Saint Adetayo sat with her trays of failed ships, each one a life she had created and extinguished. Was this hubris, she wondered? Was she taking on a role humans were never meant to have—creator and destroyer of new life?*

No. That was all wrong. She scribbled over it until the lines were just a black block on the page. The sides of her hands were covered in graphite dust.

Hagiographies had a structure. There were conventions. Sister Lucia had never considered herself a great artist—her writings would never make a person weep with beauty—but she knew the form. Saints did not wonder if they were committing a great sin in hagiographies. Saints in hagiographies were guided by God's loving hand. Real life might have been messier, but the point of stories was not their realism.

Sister Lucia took a deep breath and resettled herself cross-legged on the ground. She reached out for the ship's flank and felt its warmth, its thick skin that held them safe inside. She lived inside a miracle. How could this ship's creation be anything but glorious? How could Saint Adetayo have felt anything but love for her creations, even when they seemed a failure?

She opened her eyes. The paper lay before her. She folded over the top so she wouldn't have to see her many false starts, but she'd crossed them out so hard that their ghostly impressions taunted her from the other side.

The problem was, she didn't understand. She had no idea how Saint Adetayo had decided she knew what God's will was. She had sat in her lab with her dead specimens and known, somehow, in her heart that this was just a setback and not a sign. Sister Lucia had no such certainty in herself. She and her sisters had a much smaller choice to make, and yet she had no idea what God wanted of them. It seemed such a tiny thing, to let the ship mate and reproduce, but it was tied so deeply to everything they had vowed.

She picked up her incomplete hagiography and tore the pages to shreds. Before she could regret it, the wind carried them away like so many seeds, out over the tents where the colonists slept and the remains of their ship waiting to be made into something new and, beyond that, the lake and singing insects there. She looked up to the darkened portholes, where her sisters slept. Or should have been sleeping. One light glowed at the end of the ship.

~

"That's a good sign." Sister Gemma held the vial up to the cold white-blue glare of the chemlight. Inside, the blood was the grayish-green of dying algae, too long outside of the ship's warm body. The dye drifted into the liquid, slow and viscous. She shook it and the vial turned pink-ish. The ship was low on iron—she would have to carry unfiltered water from the lake tomorrow to replenish its hard minerals. But its antibodies were strong. "Aren't you supposed to be sleeping?"

Sister Lucia drew another vial of blood from the exposed muscle beneath the peeled-back membrane. She took a deep breath before she plunged the needle in. A ship's muscle was like cold gelatin—it felt nothing like drawing blood from a person, Sister Gemma knew. "Aren't you?"

"This would be my working shift, were we in flight. I find it easier to keep the schedule." Just a small lie.

"I—kept thinking about the ship. I kept thinking about . . . its desires, like it was a person. But that's not right. And then I thought about it like a tool for us to bend to our will, but that isn't correct either. I go around and around. I thought I should make myself useful."

Sister Gemma understood. The ship felt like another sister. It cared for them; how could they not love it? How could they not want it to be happy, and fulfilled, and to feel as loved as they felt it loved them? *You would not be asking these questions of a dairy cow,* she reminded herself.

"I've also found myself uncertain." About so much,

these days.

On the workbench they had lined up a row of tissue culture plates, where Lluviu virus and Reston and the yet-unnamed Martian virus that caused black nosebleeds were replicating. This was their small project together. Liveships had highly adaptable immune systems to shake off diseases before they carried them between atmospheres. No one really knew the mechanism behind it—so much of their anatomy was still a mystery. When she'd first come on board, Sister Lucia had spent hours watching Sister Gemma care for the ship. Months in, she'd suggested that they might use the ship's immune mechanisms to cure human disease. It was just outlandish enough to be a good hobby, and Sister Gemma had agreed.

They'd set themselves a high bar—they wanted to make an antiviral for ringeye. It was a disease from the last days of the war. A hemorrhagic, neurological fever. Victims became first aggressive, their bodies turning to tight coils of rage. In the early days, before word of the disease traveled, more people were killed by ringeye victims than by the virus. Then they began to bleed, their gums and cuts and the small veins in their lungs leaking blood until they drowned or exsanguinated. And from the pupil out, their eyes filled with concentric circles of orange and pink and black, like the rings of the planet where it had first appeared.

Whole worlds had died bleeding. Even now, when everyone knew not to go within a hundred thousand meters of an outbreak, there were stories of whole colonies going dark only to be found in puddles of their own unclotted blood. The worst part was the little children. The disease took their parents and older siblings, and left them to starve helpless and alone among the bodies.

She and Sister Lucia had had several minor successes with related diseases, though of course they did not dare seek out a sample of ringeye to bring on board. What had begun as a hobby had turned into a real hope. And they worked so well together—Sister Gemma had always considered herself an immensely practical person, while Sister Lucia was given to incredible insights and leaps of faith.

Her tablet chimed. A new message icon. She could not open it here. Sister Lucia would never pry but surely her face would give her away. She could barely school her features into a semblance of calm as it was.

"Excuse me," she said. "I'll be back in a moment."

Sister Lucia was bent over her test tube, carefully portioning drops of a reacting agent into each one. Her tongue jutted out from between her teeth. She was so engrossed, she didn't even nod. Sister Gemma took her tablet and went to the lavatory, where she could have some privacy without arousing suspicion. She perched on the edge of the sink and cradled the tablet in her lap. She didn't dare drop it. Such delicate instrumentation was likely beyond even Sister Faustina's ability to repair without the resources of a large station. And her hands were slick with sweat.

My dearest Gemma, the letter began. Sister Gemma closed her eyes. Such informality. Such intimacy, in just three words. She trembled before it. It shook her right down to the atoms of her soul.

Already her mind was betraying her by crafting a response. *Dearest.* So many doors were opened by a word like *dearest.* So many tantalizing possibilities. *Sweetest,* if she were braver. *Fondest,* perhaps. Fondest was a good word. The roots of it were in words like *infatuated* and *foolish.* How appropriate. That's what she was—an infatuated fool.

She made herself open her eyes. *I know your vocation,* the message read, *And I apologize if I am too forward in this letter. My mother used to tell me I'd have more of a mind if I didn't speak it quite so often. But I never did listen well. If you do not want to hear from me after this, I will respect that. My dearest, I have come to care for you—*

—more than care for you— Her heart skipped in her chest.

—*over the course of our correspondence.*

She hugged the tablet against herself and the heat from the battery warmed her through, like another person's head resting against her shoulder. There was more, three more paragraphs, but she couldn't stand them. She needed just a moment. If she tried to continue she would burst out of her skin.

Someone rang the bell on the door. She jumped and closed the message. "Occupied!"

"I'm sorry for interrupting." Sister Lucia.

Sister Gemma shoved down a flash of irritation. There was no reason for that. She was the one doing wrong. She pressed her face against her shirt and hoped she was merely blotchy. She ran the faucet for too long and pressed wet hands against her eyes until she saw sparks. Then she closed the message on her tablet and hid it away in a warren of descending file names about the ship's hormone levels and salt intake, where no one would ever look. She would read the rest later, alone, when she was supposed to be sleeping.

"Are you all right?" Sister Lucia asked. She held one of the cell cultures. "You look peaked."

The smile on Sister Gemma's face threatened to snap. Her teeth clicked against each other. "I have a bit of a headache. It's nothing to worry over."

"This might make you feel better." Sister Lucia lifted the tray. Inside, a tangle of lab-grown human veins sat pink and healthy and clotting. "It cured the Reston!"

Sister Gemma's breath stopped. She stared at the ventricles, the wash of fluid in the bottom of the dish. How could she think about leaving, when there was so much here to do?

～

The Reverend Mother sat on her bed, in her chamber, under the crucifix, praying. She was supposed to be asking for guidance in the matter of the ship and its imprinting on a mate. And what a theological tangle—could a consecrated house be allowed to mate, be fertilized, give birth? Or to seed another? It was a hermaphrodite species—many of its evolutionary cousins did not even require a mate. No matter their decision, scholars back in Rome would debate it for years with increasingly esoteric justifications.

Not so very long ago she had loved those debates, their citations and countercitations, their appeals to history and linguistics and textual analysis. If she were another person, with another past, she would have tried to stay in the Vatican as a scholar.

Though if she had another past, she would not have chosen this life at all. Her bones missed the gravity of her youth. Ship gravity was different. She told her sisters

45

she was from an orbital station in the second system, and that she had only done her novitiate on Earth, but that wasn't true. No matter how often people told her that ships' gravity was the same as on Earth, she felt the difference. Her body did not connect so surely to the ground beneath her feet.

The Reverend Mother had not spoken aloud in forty-three years. Even now, with only her creator to hear, she prayed in sign language. In the early years, she had been so afraid of slipping. So afraid of uttering a word and realizing a stranger was within earshot. Now her past was forty years gone, along with most of those who had known her, and she had lived more of her life silent than speaking. It was a strange thing, to realize you were no longer the person you were.

The trouble was, the past was returning.

It bubbled up inside her in the strangest of times. Standing with her sisters in the chapel, she sometimes turned to them and saw not Gemma and Lucia and Ewostatewos and Faustina and Mary Catherine and the others, but long-dead friends. The sisters' names were overwritten with the names of her novitiate class, or those of the sisters who had been on board the *Saint Afra's Tears,* her first convent. Some nights, she woke and was sixteen again, a London girl before the Fall, looking out a window on a city of a billion people. It took so long, these days, to come back to herself and realize those were stars out the glass and not millions and millions of lights from all the people living on top of each other. Sometimes it took until breakfast for her to remember herself.

When she had accepted the posting to the newly consecrated *Our Lady of Impossible Constellations,* the Reverend Mother had intended to die aboard this ship. She had intended to lead her sisters until her heart gave out aiding some plague-stricken asteroid crew or when a gravity-less hour finally let a stroke into her brain.

But now she knew—her mind was vanishing.

"Lord," she signed. She had the same crucifix in her chamber as they had in the chapel. This one she had carried with her from her novitiate in her small allotment of personal items. The faces on this batch had come out poorly. Jesus barely had a mouth, and not even the suggestion of a nose. She had taken it in like a stray. Back then, she'd had an exile's affection for misshapen things. "Tell me what to do. I don't know anymore. I barely know myself anymore, some days."

She had hidden her losses so far. So many words took her a moment to dredge up in sign language, and that moment saved her over and over from saying what she shouldn't. Someone would notice soon. Maybe they would chalk it up to the inevitable decline of age, but if it continued, there would be no denying she was not fit for her post. She wasn't familiar anymore with where they sent sisters no longer able to carry out their duties. She would not be allowed to stay aboard the ship. Ships had no allowance for dead weight. Even on orbital stations—some of which were so large they were nearly moons—the margins for water and nitrogen recycling were so thin that they would not carry an extraneous old woman.

When she was on board the *Saint Afra's Tears,* a sister had retired because her arthritis had gotten too bad for her hands to work the airlock release in an emergency evacuation. That was thirty years ago, but the only place to go was back to her family, or to the homes run by Rome on Earth. The Reverend Mother had no family. After the war, London was a crater. The moon was split by rebellion. Like so many she had scattered—

That wasn't true.

She was only allowed to tell herself true stories now, she'd decided. She couldn't allow her mind to twist upon itself any more than it already was.

She hadn't scattered, she had run. She had run from all of the things she should have been held responsible for. For decades afterward, her face had been on posters alongside the likes of General Frederick Lee, the Butcher of Mars, and President Shen, the Destroyer. No one she knew from those days would look for her among the religious. The idea of her *being* religious would have been an absurd joke. They all believed she was dead now. For years she had tried her damnedest to die, taking postings in colonies stricken with ringeye and moons still strewn with unexploded mines. By some cruel intervention, she had not. She had lived through the plagues and the bombings and the little skirmishes that no one called "war" for fear it would reignite the galaxy-spanning horror so freshly ended.

Overhead, seven bells chimed. She had used up all her time spiraling. Soon it would be breakfast and time to officiate the weddings and baptize the baby, and she would have to act as if she were whole.

Who could she tell? Lucia? Lucia was so sweet, so kind and dedicated, and she was a doctor. She would do what she was asked and tell no one. She would try to think of a solution. But she was also too kind, too much in love with everything and everyone around her. She would do what was kindest, and not what was needed.

Faustina would make the hard choices. But while she had pragmatism in spades, her heart lacked the unnamed quality that Lucia had, the ability to be guided by only instinct and love.

Gemma? In months past, she might have gone to their biologist. But something was wrong with Gemma. She had come to the *Our Lady of Impossible Constellations* so young, a wide-eyed novice with fingertips stained green from shipyard work and not a thing to hide. Now, the Reverend Mother could feel her closing in on herself, protecting some secret newly blossomed. In the romantic dramas that traveling ships transmitted back and forth to each other, sisters like them were supposed to carry no secrets. They were all supposed to be wide-eyed and innocent, waiting to be swept up by a dashing salvager or chemlight trader. That wasn't true. Wherever there were people, there were secrets.

~

This moon had no predators. Birds with long necks sang at dusk and dawn, a sound like a woman whistling through her teeth. It wasn't attractive, exactly. But it was birdsong unlike any other Sister Gemma had heard. She lay awake in the warm night listening to them swoop low over the pond, cry out, and pluck small fishes from the water. A whistle, a splash, a contented cry. Somewhere in the grasses, their nests lay hidden, and the birds would return to feed their young the meat of the fish they had chewed for them. Life from death, as it always was and always would be.

In the morning, she helped the three brides dress. This was another duty she doubted would have been done by her foremothers, but they were shorthanded, and the other colonists were needed for the actual work of turning a grassland into homes. One bride had brought an antique dress, bright blue in the style of a century ago, with small silver buttons up her spine that Sister Gemma did up one by one.

The bride had gathered thin grasses from the edge of the pond. She and her husband would wind them around each other's wrists. An old custom, to marry them to the land as much as to each other. The grass would be dried and framed above their marriage bed. Sister Gemma had heard there was a pagan rite back on Old Earth that was similar, but she was not enough of a theologist to tell if they were related.

The bride bent her head down so that Sister Gemma could slip the last lentil-sized button through its loop. She rubbed the grasses between her hands, discarding the small broken ones she found. They were of an age, and as Sister Gemma did up the buttons, she felt dizzyingly like this was her own body she was dressing. A body from a different life.

"I never thought this would happen," the bride said. She finished picking the broken grasses from her bouquet and let them go.

"Marriage?" Sister Gemma asked. One of the woman's hairs had loosed from pins and tangled in the top button;

Sister Gemma worked it free with fingers practiced from sewing her old habit back together.

"All of it," the bride said. "I love all of these people. I would give my life for any of them. I love this world even though I've only met it. I want to care for it so it will love me back. I have not had a life like that, Sister. Even three years ago I couldn't have imagined this."

"I understand," Sister Gemma said. "It's so hard to contemplate the future. It's so hard to imagine we can be anything other than what we are."

She realized her fingers were shaking against the nape of the woman's neck, and she tugged on the waistline of the dress instead, to smooth the wrinkles.

The Reverend Mother led the ceremony, of course, with Sister Lucia translating. Lucia would be a Mother Superior herself someday, Sister Gemma thought. She was full of conviction. It gave her every step gravity. You could see it, in the way her voice did not waver when she read the marriage vows for each couple to repeat and in how she smiled at each of them like they were precious and blessed. Not a cloud crossed the sky the whole morning, and the sun and fields looked like they rolled on 'til the edge of the universe.

After the ceremony, all the colonists stripped down to their underclothes and threw themselves into the pond in a laughing, shrieking, screaming tangle of limbs and grins. Even the baby came, strapped against Joseph's back, squalling when his toes hit the cold water.

"Oh my," Sister Mary Catherine said.

"Oh, hush." Sister Gemma watched from far enough back to call it a respectful distance. "Don't look if you don't want. We're all made in His image, you know. There are some sects in the fourth system that conduct services in the nude, because they believe that is how He intended us to live."

"Life is a rich tapestry," Sister Mary Catherine said and turned, primly, back to stirring the pot of chickpea-flour stew they would be feasting on in a few hours. Sister Faustina was setting up tents for the newlywed couples, scraped together from their ship's emergency evac kit and the colonists' extra sheets. After tonight, they would share tents again until the houses were built, but they deserved privacy on their first wedded night. Sister Lucia, so expert with a scalpel, had butchered the lizards and was roasting them skin-on over a fire built from real wood for the smoke. Their fat dripped down their golden meat and hissed in the embers. What a feast it would be, what a night it was.

~

All lovely things had to end of course, like the most beautiful of sunsets harkening a night cold enough to slice through flesh right into bone. The sisters reboarded the *Our Lady of Impossible Constellations* come morning, sent off with a sack of barley flour as a donation. As they lifted off, the fields and colonists shrank to the size of aphids, then the moon became a distant green speck, and then vanished entirely. The ship was impatient with the delay. It would not stay to the speed that Sister Ewostatewos asked of it and it pulled at the reins, edging them into the top-speed range, where the walls shuddered with its effort. You could feel it heaving, if you leaned against the softest places in the deepest rooms of it, the thudding great heart working to pump hemolymphatic fluid through a body as great as the grand beasts of Old Earth myth, those long-dead whales and elephants and apatosauruses.

Before they began their gravity-fast, the sisters held chapel. Sister Lucia read the gospels and Sister Mary Catherine led them in song. They had new music to play, which had come from a relay system near the last moon and claimed to be an organ recital from before humanity took to the stars. Their liturgical calendar was eleven years old. Perhaps, Sister Faustina thought, as her voice rose with the second chorus of "Lord of the Dance," this new priest the Church was sending to bring them to heel would have one. They still varied the liturgical seasons based on the turns of the Earth. Every few years another debate began about simply making a standardized, static calendar for use across the four systems. But those debates were as likely to succeed as the idea of heliocentrism in the age of Galileo.

The Reverend Mother passed communion wafers among them and Sister Lucia gave her the Bible to read the next passage from. Sister Faustina watched the Reverend Mother closely, but she seemed herself again. For now. Last night, when Sister Faustina was awake at the communications array, she'd heard the old woman thrashing in her sleep.

At the end of service, they turned off the gravity. The books were strapped down or put into cabinets. Sister Ewostatewos rubbed her hands across the moss on the walls of the chapel to seal the crucifix and the Stations of the Cross tightly to the wall once more. One by one they dispersed, pulling themselves along the handholds grown into the walls and floor and ceiling.

Sister Faustina did not strap herself down when the gravity went off. She preferred the feel of it—on the world where she was born, the gravity was two-thirds of Earth Standard. The company that owned them had given all the children vitamin and hormone injections to grow the bones and muscles of Earthers, so they would be better miners. But Earth Standard Gravity still weighed heavy on her shoulders, like she was dragging an anchor. Two years ago was the last time the *Our Lady of Impossible Constellations* had docked at a moon with a similar gravity to that of her childhood, and when the rest of the sisters were sleeping in their chambers she had left the ship in her vacsuit skin instead of her habit and sprinted across the plains until the night air burned in her lungs, each leap taking her yards away.

II.

Sententia probabilis

SISTER LUCIA FOLLOWED THE Reverend Mother back
from services. Her eyes were full of grit. She had slept
little while they had been moored on the colony-moon.
As she got older, she found that atmospheres and hori-
zons disquieted her. Now, back on the ship, the tiredness
crashed over her in one unbreaking wave.

The Reverend Mother paused, gripping the handhold,
her feet in their stickboots trailing out behind her. The hall
was wide enough to pass, but Sister Lucia waited for her.
Perhaps she had had an epiphany about the ship. They were
getting so close to the point when they would have to shift
its trajectory. Ships like these weren't like deadships—at
speed they could only make subtle turns, and they couldn't
afford to burn so much fuel on stopping to make a sharp
turn.

The Reverend Mother looked behind her, at Lucia.
Her mouth was half-open, tempting speech. Her hand
slipped on the bar until she was holding on to it with

only her fingertips.

"Mother?" Sister Lucia asked. "Did you forget something?" Perhaps she needed water. Sister Lucia's own grandmother, in her dotage, had been stricken with sudden and desperate thirsts. Such were the indignities of age.

The Reverend Mother licked her lips, and her tongue moved like she was trying to form a word. A chill struck Sister Lucia right in the coils of her guts and ran icily up her back. She did not know why the Mother Superior had taken a vow of silence. None of them did. She had heard that the Reverend Mother had been silent even on the first day of her novitiate. Whatever the cause, it was not a vow meant to be broken.

"Mother," she said, and let go of her own handhold to reach for her.

The Mother Superior recoiled. Her hand flashed a sign—what was that? It was clumsy, the gestures blurring into each other and distorted by her shaking.

"I don't understand," Lucia said. "I'm sorry, please tell me again. Are you all right?"

"Please," the Reverend Mother signed. "I understood too late. Please. You must forgive me."

Sister Lucia paused. Something told her she should not go closer just yet. She pressed her hand against the wall and the moss grew to hold her in place. "Forgive what?"

The Reverend Mother shrank back against the wall. The moss reacted as it was supposed to in zero-gravity, licking at her feet to try to hold her still. The Reverend Mother jumped and banged against the ceiling, trying to get away from its reaching fingers. "You must forgive me."

"You just had a moment of confusion, Mother . . . perhaps we should get you a cup of tea? It's been a tiring few days."

"You must forgive me. You must forgive me. You must forgive me . . ." The words blended into each other, her fingers losing their dexterity. Sister Lucia caught only fragments—*I was a fool* and *I did not know how cruel they were* and like a chorus, *please please please.*

"Mother!" Sister Lucia grabbed her arm. She had to make her stop, something was very wrong, she would hurt herself like this—

The Reverend Mother reared back and sent herself spiraling down the hall, clawing against the walls. She wasn't turning herself the right way to stall her momentum in the lack of gravity. Sister Lucia shouted, despite herself, and panic flared in the Reverend Mother's eyes. A hatch opened—Sister Faustina, flying out from the communications chamber. She saw the Reverend Mother and caught her around the middle, her other arm twisted through the handle on the hatch. She grunted when her arm snapped back with the force of the Reverend Mother's inertia.

"Lucia!" Sister Faustina snapped, forgetting the honorific. Sister Lucia bristled, but there was no time for their animosity. "What on all the earths—?"

"I don't know!"

Sister Faustina looked at the Reverend Mother, shivering like a wet cat against her. The old woman's hands were still and silent, and in her eyes . . . they were lacking something, some essential light.

"Come, Mother," Sister Faustina said, softly, like she was talking to a feverish child. She pushed herself off from the wall, floated lightly past Sister Lucia, and opened the hatch of the Reverend Mother's chamber. She was not a gentle woman by nature, but she was careful as she worked the straps to hold the Reverend Mother in her bed. The light was flowing back into the Mother's eyes. She blinked like she was freshly waking.

"Sister Faustina?" She looked down at the straps holding her in her bed and frowned. Her signing was fluid and legible again. "What?"

Sister Faustina looked at Sister Lucia and stepped back.

"You had . . . a fit, Mother. You were—very upset."

The Reverend Mother's hands clenched, but when she signed, she said, "I'm only tired—it's been a long time since we stood under a sun for so many hours. I'll just sleep."

"Mother, you were asking for forgiveness."

"All us mortals need forgiveness, child. Let me be, I feel much better now."

"But—" Sister Lucia began. "Wouldn't you rather have me bring my medical bag and have a look at you?" But Sister Faustina took her hand and pulled her away.

When the hatch had sealed behind them, Sister Faustina rubbed her shoulder and grimaced. Muscle strain, from stopping the Reverend Mother's fall. Sister Lucia would prescribe some painkillers out of their stores.

"I don't understand it," Sister Lucia said. Her legs worked uselessly. She wished for gravity, so she could pace.

"Don't you, though? You're a doctor."

"I don't get your meaning." She had never liked Sister Faustina, so curt and sharp-tongued, so willing to dispense with the rules of their order. Did no one else see how she made only the barest motions of performing her obligations?

"Don't you? An elderly woman whose mannerisms have changed, who loses her words, who seems to become unstuck from time and place more and more often? You are with her the most of all of us. You are her voice more often than not. Is this really the first time you've noticed?"

Sister Lucia looked away. It was not, of course. The small signs had been building for months.

"What would you diagnose, if she were any other patient?"

"Early-stages dementia. Alzheimer's maybe. I would have to run more tests. She'll never submit to them."

"Of course." Sister Faustina tapped the soles of her boots together and the little suckers emerged from the bottom. She pressed her feet into the wall to plant herself. "What is the procedure for this?"

"Now? I'm not sure. We will have to contact the Vatican, surely. She will likely be removed from the ship, if I deem her no longer capable of fulfilling her spiritual duties. There's a rest home on Earth, and the moon. A few in the second system too."

"And then we'll be assigned a new Mother Superior?"

"We would elect one, if she died without warning. I think if the Vatican is involved in her retirement they may choose to assign us a tenured sister from another convent. It would be up to them."

Sister Faustina hissed through her teeth. "What a perfect opportunity."

"What?"

"Come with me." Sister Faustina pulled her into the communications room and handed over her headphones. Sister

Lucia slipped them over her head, hesitantly, but when she read the cardinal's message she understood.

"When did you receive this?"

"A few days ago."

"What did the Mother Superior have to say about it?"

Sister Faustina was silent.

"You didn't tell her."

"As you said, today was not the first sign that something is wrong. I haven't answered it."

"It isn't up to you to decide what to do!"

"You're right. It's up to us, now."

She was insane. The woman was patently insane. "If this is the Church's will, we must follow it. You know that."

"Even if it's regressive? Even if it's a sly attempt by Central Governance to worm their way back across the four systems?"

"The Church is not an arm of Central Governance—"

"Isn't it? Maybe it wasn't for a while, but I've been digging into our new Pontifex. Orders across the three outlying systems are alarmed, Lucia. The old pope died alone in his gardens and they buried him in a week. The new pope is a cousin of Shen—*that* Shen. And several other cardinals have had quick and quiet burials in the past years. It would be so easy for them to slip this past us. Everyone is so scattered now. We didn't even hear about this new pope until the old one was a year dead, we're so far out. And I assure you there will be orders that don't hear about these priests they're sending until one arrives on their doorstep."

"We are meant to be obedient, Sister. Even when we don't understand. It was in those vows you seem to care so little for. And if you wanted a religion where men and women of the religious life had the same level of authority, you should have been a Lutheran."

"I have lived by my vows every moment of my life since I took them. Do not accuse me of disobedience just because you are a starry-eyed saint-worshipper."

"It's not just about the motions—"

"This is not an argument about theology!" Sister Faustina was red-faced, sweat collecting damp around the line of her wimple. She'd slammed her hand into the communications console and the moss on it had grown up around her fist, thinking the force for turbulence. "You know something is very wrong. Use your brain, Lucia. This is not right. And if we tell the Vatican about our dear Mother Superior's failing mind, they will rip her from her home, leave her on some unfamiliar planet, and send a pliant priest to make us missionaries of Central Governance."

Sister Lucia did not want to believe it. She held her vows so close in her heart and she had never, ever questioned them. She had followed God to disease-stricken dying colonies, into asteroid belts still spread with mines from the war, and out here to an edge of space with so few people that if they got into trouble, rescue would never come in time. She had not questioned. It was not her place. And yet, she also knew her history. Religion was a useful arm of the state, often enough. What better way to crush resistance than to own the souls of the people? What better way to spread your government than to tie it to the name of God?

She pressed her hands against her eyes. "What do we do?"

"We can play dumb about the message—pretend we never received it. That will work until this priest arrives. It will give us a few months, hopefully. We will have to talk to the Mother Superior when she's in a more stable mood. At the least, we will have to remove her authority to open the airlocks. I don't want to get blown out into the vacuum if she has an episode. In the long term? I don't know. This will progress."

"We will have to call another quorum. Ask our sisters' opinions. I'm sure if we approach it with sensitivity, the Reverend Mother will understand we only want to help. She's just frightened. She has never liked appearing weak, you know."

Sister Faustina shook her head. "If we tell Sister Mary

Catherine, she won't understand. She's planetbound in her soul, I think. And—there is something happening with the Reverend Mother that's not just the paranoia of her disease. She's always been afraid of something, and this is making it worse."

"I know." Sister Lucia leaned against the wall, and let the ship's muscle cushion her. "We can't ask. It's not just that she wouldn't tell us. She abandoned that life when she took her vows and her religious name. Whatever ghosts she carries, it is not our business, and it would be a grave transgression to ask."

"I wonder what she wanted forgiveness for."

"We're all sinners."

Sister Faustina chuckled. "Not like the Reverend Mother, apparently." She saw the look on Sister Lucia's face and stopped. "I mean no disrespect. As you said, it was a different life."

"We can tell Sister Gemma." Yes, that was the solution. She was a practical person. How still her hands were, when she cut into the very ship that bore them all safely through these vast and cruel darknesses, a ship that could expel them all with one breath from its prodigious lungs, like so many meddlesome bacteria! She was a woman of duty, Sister Gemma.

Sister Faustina had turned away from her and fiddled silently with the arcane dials on the communications array. Sister Lucia felt the cupful of belief she was holding tightly inside her tremble, and tip, and spill. "Yes. Sister Gemma is a very intelligent woman. I'm sure she will understand our dilemma here."

"What's wrong?"

"Nothing." Her voice was flat. "I consider Sister Gemma a great friend."

"You do like your secrets." She spat it, but Sister Faustina did not even turn.

~

It was easier for Sister Gemma to access some parts of the ship when the gravity was off and she weighed less heavily against its soft insides. She latched the helmet onto the neck ring of her suit and slipped the glass faceplate down until the seal hissed and the air went from tasting fresh to tasting like the inside of a can.

She had to wear a breathing mask, for the ship's natural gases were preserved in these parts for the health of its organs. The methane stink made its way through the filter still. It reminded her of a station they'd visited for refueling that still raised cattle in a herd, for an "artisanal" meat supply, rather than scaffolding layers of protein on cell lattices in laboratories like most stations did. The cattle were half-crazed, banging their heads against padded walls and bellowing at the UV lights that were meant to mimic Old Earth sun but that clearly did not fool the animals' primitive hind-brain. Cows were stupid, slow, lumbering creatures, but they understood their environment. Colonies that raised cattle had to breed small herds over generations for them to acclimate to the changes in gravity, air pressure, and atmosphere mix. They were only of the world, and so small changes to it disturbed them more. The stationmaster of that ag-station had told the sisters that all cows made that much noise, but in their moaning Sister Gemma had only heard grief. She'd longed for someone to put them out of their misery. Only a month later, they received word that the entire herd had died of an unknown neurological disease. They had frothed at the mouth and bashed themselves against the walls until the terrified bovine vet shot them all lest they stampede and slaughter the population or knock the station from orbit.

This passage was tighter than it had been when she'd delivered the immunizations. She had to squeeze her hips through taut muscle before she reached the other valve that opened into the central cavity.

As soon as she was through, she saw why. The ovo-testis was swollen with eggs. They stretched the thin membrane, each the size of a child's fist and shimmering light orange. There must be hundreds. Sister Gemma checked the ones she could see. All looked well-formed and symmetrical. She didn't see any half-developed eggs (a sign of a nutrient deficiency) or graying infected ova. It would be a healthy litter if it were allowed to fertilize. She pressed her faceplate against the egg closest to the surface. The nutrient-rich yolk inside shimmered darkly under the harsh light from her helmet. The eggs lit up one by one as her headlamp swung past them, carpeting the inner tract, up along the ship's central nervous system, down the curve of sinew supporting its guts. Not long now. If they did not allow the *Our Lady of Impossible Constellations* to fertilize her eggs they would need to coax her to expel them before they expired inside her and left a raging infection.

Unlike most gastropods, the ships could not self-fertilize. They had been bred that way, so that shipwrights could more easily control their lines. Usually shipwrights would rub one ship with the pheromones of its intended mate to trigger egg production and mating hormones. Out here the distance between ships was usually too vast for them to be attracted naturally. Sister Gemma touched the swollen sac to see if she could check the number of eggs. As soon as she stretched it taut the whole ship shuddered.

"Sorry, girl," she said, and rubbed the muscle until it turned a healthy dark green, hot with blood.

She had intended to check the rest of the inner systems now. Ships were not prone to many diseases—few things could infect them, and they came across others of their kind so rarely—but there were some rare neurological and pulmonary conditions that could develop as they reached maturity. The egg sac was blocking her easy access to those systems. She could cut through the mucus membranes here if she wanted, but that was such trauma for a routine examination. Instead, she tucked herself into a twist of muscle between an artery and the eggs and pulled out her tablet again. She was alone here. She had prepared herself. It was time.

Again her eyes caught on *Dearest* and fire bloomed beneath her ribs.

It had started a year ago, this dangerous, disastrous, delicious dalliance. They had docked at the same station as the *Cheng I Sao,* listed on the manifests as a deadship with a cargo of chemlights and water treatment tablets. Sister Gemma had been standing at the porthole looking out when they came abreast of her, and she had seen the flesh mixed with metal, the long waving appendages that trickled through the solar winds like their own ship's frills. At first she had been horrified—what sick twisting of nature was this, what grave mutilation of a living being?—and yet she could not draw herself away.

The sisters met the crew of the *Cheng I Sao* in the corridors of the station, next to a stall selling sticky rice paste fried to gloriously brown crisps, where one of the station operators could observe their trade as was custom. Sister Gemma saw the engineer immediately. She was a small, compact woman, clearly born on a planet with punishing gravity. Hexidecimal code tattoos scattered themselves down her arms from shoulder to elbow. That had been a fashion among helium miners. She did not smile, not even when her captain told a long, opaque joke about seaweed nutrient drink and moondust that clearly made sense only to the crew. She was an asteroid in the form of a woman, and Sister Gemma was fascinated.

They had stayed in the station a week, pumping unrecyclable waste out of the ship and repairing all the metal parts that were far overdue for their regular maintenance. Her sisters spent that time in prayer or ministry. Sister Gemma, shamefully (so shamefully, her face burned still when she thought of herself slipping away from the ship in the morning like she had no duties at all, no obligations) had spent it with the engineer. Her name was Vauca, a name twisted from the Latin roots of the absent place they lived. She said her parents were strange pagans who worshipped the stars and the dark. She did not know much about them; they had died young of plague.

She showed Sister Gemma her ship. She had bought a

litter of failed shiplings from a shipyard station—the small ones that were usually euthanized, that wouldn't grow the inner chambers necessary to house humans—and coaxed them into growing into lattices welded to the outside of a deadship.

"I've gotten them to propel us," she had said. "It's far more cost-effective than engine fuel. But making jumps is just a dream—we still have to use a hyperspace engine for that. And they keep dying on me. I wish we had someone with your expertise aboard."

Sister Gemma had not been in love, not yet. But she was in awe of the project. What a grand experiment! A colony of unformed ships, working together! Purposeless beings given purpose in community! And of course, she was in awe of Vauca, too.

They had not met again. Twice the *Our Lady of Impossible Constellations* had arrived at stations where the *Cheng I Sao* had been docked before them, and small packages were waiting for Sister Gemma. Not gifts, of course. She was not allowed to accept gifts. A vial of one of the shiplings' hemolymphatic fluid with a note asking for her opinion on a strange genetic marker. A packet of nitrogen supplements specifically formatted for a maturing ship, difficult to find in this system. *I remember you were looking for these.* Sister Gemma had left things in return at other stations—a medicine to try on a dying shipling, fluid from her own ship for comparison, a small rock worn flat in a river on a gorgeous agricultural moon that she thought Vauca would like.

And of course, they exchanged letters. Dozens. She was careful to wait a proper time before writing back, or it might have been hundreds. Their correspondence was jumbled, asynchronous, with letters bouncing across hundreds of relay satellites to be received late and out of order and corrupted by distance. She longed to hear Vauca's words in the order they were intended. She had learned to long for small things in this shipbound life—the crunchy skin of a fresh apple right as it split beneath your teeth, air that tasted like salt and decay smelled from the bank of a stagnant estuary, a dear one's conversation unbroken.

"I don't know what to do," she said to the eggs surrounding her. For she loved this ship too, and the life she had on it, every month spent under a new sky doing as much good as her two hands could do. She loved its strange biology and the revelations it showed her. She imagined that decades ago, when humanity was confined to its single sphere, she would have been a scientist and spent her life pursuing the great creation of beasts like this.

Here in the central cavity the air was warmer, holding her close and safe. The ship's heartbeat echoed through her body in great waves, like she was kneeling in an ocean, letting the surf crash over her again and again and again. She rocked with the sound. Time was once, she heard God's voice in this body. Not in words—she was no saint and did not want to be—but in the mysterious workings of it, its infallibility, the great work they did on board. Somehow, she had started seeing it as only an animal again. Beautiful, yes, and an extraordinary testament to human ingenuity. But she saw God in the faces of Terret and her child, and the pulsing engines of deadships and the stars themselves, just as much as she saw Him here, now. She couldn't decide if that was because she had stopped looking for Him here, or because He was showing her that she could find Him anywhere she went.

~

At the second quorum, they chose to leave the gravity off. It made everything feel quieter, even though they all knew that sound waves traveled just as well without gravity's hold. Sister Lucia let herself drift in the currents of the ship's exhalations.

"Today is the last day where we can alter the ship's course without burning into our fuel reserves," she said. She had brought her Bible with her, and held it tucked under her arm, like one of the passages might illuminate this strange conflict they found themselves in. "We shall decide by supermajority."

"Let us go one by one," said Sister Mary Catherine, who everyone knew had not changed her mind and never would. "So we each may be heard."

"Go on then." Sister Faustina floated cross-legged by the door. "Try not to be too hyperbolic."

The Revered Mother's hand jabbed the air—a quick censure—and she fell silent.

"This is holy house. How would you justify this perversion of its purity?"

"Were we a convent on a new colony, we would breed livestock for food and labor for our parish. It is the ship's nature to seek and reproduce. Let the animal do as it will."

Sister Mary Catherine huffed, but she had had her turn. Sister Ewostatewos too came down on the side of allowing the ship to do as it would, though she pointed out the ship was hardly a natural animal. Sister Varvara, always one for dramatics, dabbed at the corners of her eyes with the edge of her wimple as she declared that she had prayed hard on this for many sleepless nights and could not condone it. What a sentimentalist, that one. No wonder she had taken the name of a woman who had died singing hymns at the bottom of a pit.

"What of you, Sister Gemma?" Sister Lucia asked.

"We've come down split so far."

Sister Gemma had hung at the edge of the group, floating above a pew like she longed to sit in it. She rubbed her hands together over and over, though it wasn't cold.

"I'm afraid I will have to abstain," she said.

"Abstain?" Sister Lucia looked at Sister Faustina, and saw no surprise at all on her face.

"You see—" Sister Gemma swallowed, and real tears did well up in her eyes. "I'm sorry. I can't continue to act as one of you. It would be dishonest, and I have been dishonest for so long. I'm leaving."

"Leaving?" Sister Varvara started, and smacked her head on the ceiling. "What do you mean, leaving? You've taken another posting in another convent?"

"Leaving the order. I've decided this isn't the life that I am called to anymore." She curled her arms around herself. "I'm sorry. You have no idea. I never thought—"

All eyes turned to the Reverend Mother. She only had one question. "Why?"

Sister Gemma looked away from the Reverend Mother and the front of the room and the crucifix and her face flushed pink. "I've fallen in love."

The room exploded.

"Love!" snapped Sister Mary Catherine. The words dripped with ice, as cold as anything on the dark side of any moon. "Romantic love? You swore an oath, my sister, how long have you been breaking it for?"

"With who?" Sister Ewostatewos asked, brow furrowed. "Who on any earth, out here? Not some shiftless metals-scavenger, oh Gemma, you know that they will tear you apart sure as anything. It isn't like the romance novels."

"You've been hiding this too?" Sister Lucia leaned in to Sister Faustina. "Don't hide it, you must have seen the communications going out. Did you tell the Reverend Mother? Do you think yourself in charge now?"

"I thought it was Sister Gemma's right to choose for herself," Sister Faustina hissed back, their voices lost among the confusion. "I have hidden nothing that you wouldn't yourself want hidden. Do you think you would want to make a choice like this with all your sisters breathing down your neck?"

"I will tell you what I think, I think you should not be the only one overseeing communications."

"Stop," the Reverend Mother signed. She floated to Gemma and placed one hand on her head. "If you wish to leave, Sister, then you have my blessing. We are fools to not follow when we are called."

"Thank you, Mother," Sister Gemma said. She wiped away the tears sparkling in the pinks of her eyes and laughed. That laugh softened something in Sister Lucia's heart. What a strange world they were in, to be on a gravid ship, to have a sister who had fallen in love, to live in this precious precarious time when all was new.

"I vote we let the ship do as it will," Sister Lucia said. "I mean, to return to the issue."

In the end they all agreed, some more begrudgingly than others. Sister Ewostatewos tracked the ship's trajectory and discovered that its mate was docked at a small station where they could trade for chemlights and sugar. They could not decide what to do about the babies, if the litter was born healthy. Even Sister Mary Catherine, now that the decision had been made, offered up her opinion that they should return the viable shiplings to Earth to be shaped for convents. It was again a silly idea (such a long journey to Earth for such a small gift) but at least she was participating.

~

After the quorum, when the shock had dissipated, Sister Faustina found Gemma in her laboratory, bent over the last slide of the ship's plasma she might ever draw.

"I haven't sent word yet," she said, when Sister Faustina sat down on the lab bench across from her. "I haven't any idea where in the system the *Cheng I Sao* is. I don't want to be disappointed just yet. It could be months before I disembark, if we don't cross paths before that."

"I see." Sister Faustina took in the lab, the small marks of Sister Gemma's time here in her handwriting on every label and the sealed cup of green tea cooling on the desk in the corner, next to a draft of a letter to the university on Venus's ninth moon about the ship's egg health. "Are you nervous?"

Sister Gemma laughed. Sister Faustina hadn't expected that at all. "I thought I would be. I thought I would spend these last nights lying sleepless in my bed, worrying that I was throwing every good thing away. But I don't. I've been so full of—certainty is the wrong word—peace, I suppose, ever since I decided. It was the same when I chose to take my vows after my novitiate. The other girls in my class spent all night praying, and I slept like a child with a warm glass of real milk." She looked down at her hands, clad in blue gloves. "I feel ready."

Sister Faustina slid her tablet across the workbench.

Sister Gemma read. It was a manifest, of ships within radius of a station.

"What's this?"

"All of the ships docked at or close to Keda Station, where the ship's mating partner is. I've been contacting ones that have supplies we need and setting up exchanges." She scrolled down the list and tapped a name there.

Sister Gemma read the line. She had to put down the slide lest she crack it in her shaking grip. For there in pure white pixels was written the name of the ship of her dearest, beloved correspondent. "How? Did you send a message ahead to them?" That was silly, of course. Even if Sister Faustina had, it would have taken the *Cheng I Sao* days to arrive here.

"Happenstance," Sister Faustina replied, though it felt like so much more than that. The air hung heavy on them both, weighted down with so much meaning. "Perhaps it was fated. A sign you've made the right choice."

"I never really believed in signs," Sister Gemma said. And yet her cheeks flushed.

"Neither do I," Sister Faustina said. "But this sure seems like one, doesn't it?" She opened a new message on the tablet and left it there for Sister Gemma, with the address set to the *Cheng I Sao*'s coordinates.

~

Keda Station was a little box of nothing in a corner of space full of nothing. No important planets or waystations, no colonies, no moons good for mining or asteroids good for netting. The station itself was a bit of space junk that someone had plucked out of a decaying orbit and set around a moon with lax property laws. Inside the station, the bar served yellowish beer that tasted like an old packet of soy protein. You had to barter for your drink, or pay hard metal. No currencies recognized.

The sisters of the *Our Lady of Impossible Constellations* pressed up against the portholes looking out over the docked ships. They and the other crew had to wait inside the station for it to begin, for ships' mating was hardly gentle and it was safer to disembark. The Reverend Mother sat primly in a chair in the quietest corner of the bar. The station's proprietor, it turned out, was a devout Catholic, and he fussed with childish glee over the first Mother Superior he'd seen since he left his home colony.

Gemma watched her sisters press up against the glass. She didn't belong with them anymore. She was wearing clothes that didn't fit her—the ones she'd given over when she took her vows had long since been converted to carbon and fed to the ship. Sister Faustina had found her a pair of men's cargo pants and a shirt meant to go under a vacsuit woven with radiation-repelling fibers. She did not feel like herself. Her head itched without its covering, and the skin on her arms prickled with gooseflesh. She still thought of herself as *Sister Gemma*. She had had another name once, but she had left that behind so long ago and been reborn. And here she was, standing in a strange station in a stranger's clothes, waiting to be reborn again.

She turned away.

Vauca (her Vauca, if she was allowed to imagine that) was waiting for her on the ramp up from the airlock. She was so much like Gemma remembered her. Strong arms, strong jaw. Hands scarred from coolant burns and plague. A smile like a slanted line.

"Hello," Vauca said. She had her hands shoved deep in her coverall pockets, but Gemma saw them twisting nervously, and her heart filled with joy for someone to be so needful of her.

When they were close enough to touch Vauca reached out and cupped Gemma's cheek. The brush of her fingertips sent frisson down Gemma's spine and she shivered. She smelled like burnt wiring and anise, engine oil and peppermint. Gemma wanted to close her eyes and breathe her in.

"Can I kiss you?"

Gemma swallowed. It had been years. More than years. A lifetime ago, an oath ago, a name ago. It was so hard to imagine. Her heart was pounding in her chest already. She took Vauca's hands and let her palms warm her. "I'd like to," she said. "I—maybe not yet?"

Vauca laughed and squeezed her hands. It was only a matter of inches for Gemma to lean her head on her shoulder where it fit so naturally. "Of course."

They stood that way for a while, two quiet bodies

among the press of people and the noise of haggling and mineral trading and the docked ships outside grating against the armatures keeping them attached to the station. Gemma thought she could stay here forever, let the dust come and turn them to statues and she would still be content.

Then a hush swept across the station, and Vauca's fine fingers gripped her hair. "Oh! Look!"

She opened her eyes. The *Our Lady of Impossible Constellations* circled the other ship, lights spiraling down the whole of its cerulean body. Its fronds waved in the airless dark, and little ice crystals followed in its wake as it exhaled excess oxygen and nitrogen. The other ship was smaller, a darker green, the color of the dried kelp that Sister Varvara bought from water-world traders to make dashi. They circled each other, closer and closer, synchronized like they were capable of speech and higher thought. The *Our Lady of Impossible Constellations* curled its head and touched the end of the other ship, which curled in to meet her equally. Mating secretions slicked their bodies and then froze and crackled away. Their bodies pulsed and shimmered, pinprick wormholes opening and closing around them with red sparking pops. It was impossible to tell one from the other now. Both their hides mottled with every green hue and their gelatinous muscles obscured where one body ended and the other began.

Gemma saw Sister Lucia wipe glittering tears from her eyes, and Sister Faustina lean forward. Even the Reverend Mother watched from her spot in the bar and Gemma thought she saw a smile. It was only right that this be so beautiful. The bodies outside glowed greener, bioluminescent trails running from fronds to head and back. The armor plates that kept them safe from meteors and dust and radiation opened like gills against the force of their great breaths, revealing the softer green and gray underneath like the bottom of a pond on a sunny day.

And just as soon as it had begun, it was over. The two ships disentangled themselves. The smaller ship slid back into its docking port with one wave of its frills, where its crew was waiting to check its nutrient levels and ply it with saline-sweet water and sucrose tablets. The *Our Lady of Impossible Constellations* stayed out beyond the tug of the station for a long few minutes, facing toward this planet's orange sun and the nebula beyond. The ships did not exhale in space, not the way humans conceived of exhaling, but Gemma thought she saw it swell and relax, like this was the first moment of peace it had had in a long time. Then it too turned and slid softly into the dock where Gemma had left its homing beacon.

~

Sister Faustina watched the ship settle back into its dock. Its calloused outer skin rippled and the plates locked back into their places. It would be a few hours before they could return. The ship would be skittish and sensitive until the last of the pheromones scattered across the solar winds. She liked this fine. She intended to find a trader from the first system, who had promised her a bottle of real, dark molasses. That was the sweetness she'd grown up with. The other sisters preferred white sugar for their refined sucrose. It had been a long time since she had tasted molasses dark like the bottom of the deepest, coldest mine shaft. But now she had been put in charge of procuring their supplies, so ha! The others would just have to live with molasses until they ran low again.

Gemma, habitless, looked taller than she had seemed before. She leaned against that engineer of hers, their arms tangled. Such youth. Let her be happy, Sister Faustina thought, to whatever god really watched over them. Hard choices should have rewards.

She watched Sister Lucia drift back toward the Reverend Mother and settle next to her in the bar. Good. Without speaking of it, they began taking shifts to watch over her, but so far it had never gotten as bad as that night. The stationmaster served the two cups of lemon barley water, and Sister Lucia smiled at him. Small kindnesses should always be rewarded. The Reverend Mother lifted her glass up to the light from the lantern hanging from the ceiling and shook it so the small barley particles swirled. Where was she really from, Sister Faustina wondered. Barley water was a childhood drink in this system, the cool sweet thing your mother gave you after a hard day in the mines or a long, sweating summer afternoon. Just enough sugar and calories to make your blood run a little hotter, just enough water to quench your thirst, and barley grew everywhere.

"Excuse me," someone said.

She turned and was met with a very young man. He barely looked old enough to shave. He was as tall as someone born in zero-g, and all legs, but his bones were strong, so he must just be a tall planet-born. He was carrying a small traveling bag, and he was dressed in all black. Around his neck he wore a priest's collar.

"Hello," he said, and extended his hand. "Are you, by chance, the sisters of the *Our Lady of Impossible Constellations*? Of the Order of Saint Rita?"

She was so startled that she could not bring herself to shake his hand.

"I'm sorry," he said, and then tried again in very slow and clumsy outer-system patois. "Do you not speak English?"

"I speak English," she snapped, and he looked genuinely crestfallen. "Who *are* you?" She knew already, of course. She had to hear it from the ass's mouth.

"Oh yes, communication is so spotty out here, isn't it! I am your new priest." He held out his hand again and this time, regrettably, she had no choice but to shake it. "What luck I found you! I feel as if I've been chasing your tail for ages. I had to pay the captain of the trawler I was on quite a bit of money to have him drop me here when I saw you were docked."

"What luck," Sister Faustina repeated hollowly, and caught Sister Lucia's eye over the priest's shoulder. "Do you have luggage, Father? Perhaps you could help me gather our supplies, and then we can take it aboard after the ship has settled."

"Oh, yes," he said, oblivious to how she was chewing the inside of her cheek to shreds. "I have several bags. It's been a long time since we've brought this system up to date with current Church practices, you know."

～

Sister Faustina and Sister Lucia stood above the clutch of eggs. After three weeks, most were now showing signs of development. Sister Faustina had never seen a tadpole, but Sister Mary Catherine had assured her the wriggling inside looked just like them. Big black eyes stared balefully at them from within the orange spheres. Amorphous tails writhed inside their nutrient baths. Some of the eggs had not been fertilized, and lay squished and dark and graying in between their lively might-have-been siblings. Soon those would be reabsorbed into the ship's body as it made space for its clutch to grow and mature. The gestation of this species was not long; in a week or two the eggs would be too large to stay safe here inside the ship. There was a shipyard in orbit around a gas giant that was two weeks away at thruster speed. Another few planets scattered closer in the system had the low-gravity/high-sunlight combination the larval shiplings would crave.

Sister Lucia knelt beside the egg sac, feeling under the membrane for the thick nerve bundle that lay beneath. "Hand me the scalpel, please."

Sister Faustina passed it. Sister Lucia carefully split the mucus seal from the muscle beneath, sweating as she squinted at it to avoid rupturing the egg sac. The eggs were far enough along now that it would not be disastrous, but they had nowhere to nurse the clutch. The sac peeled up and Sister Lucia pressed a thermometer underneath, and then a gas spectrometer.

"Everything seems to be in order," she said. "What I wouldn't give for Gemma right now. Though I don't think she was an expert on this bit, either."

"Shipwrights guard their secrets close. And how many

ships are allowed to imprint on a wild mate?"

Sister Lucia shook her head, and wiped a smear of gelatinous fluid off her face mask and onto her pant leg. The two of them had come to an understanding. The fragile alliance they had formed that terrible night in the Reverend Mother's quarters had deepened these past several weeks. They were not friends, but they were comrades, and co-conspirators, and currently the two people keeping this ship running as it should. Sister Lucia knelt close to the eggs again and the big, half-developed eyes nearest her fluttered. One of them was smaller than the others, more yellow than orange. She laid her hand over it through the membrane. "Look at that one—so small. What a tiny baby. Who knew they had runts in these litters?"

"You're too sentimental," Sister Faustina said. Ships were closer to octopi or deep-sea monsters than dogs. Though they *were* cute at this stage. In the way bubble-eyed children's toys were cute. "It'll get eaten, you know. If we were a shipyard, we'd throw all the ones that didn't look promising out into the vacuum to suffocate as soon as they broke their eggshells."

"Shush," Sister Lucia said to the eggs and the wrigglers inside. "Don't listen to her. We believe in all of you."

"They're invertebrates, Lucia," Sister Faustina said. One of the eyes inside an egg hanging right by her head blinked at her, as if in reproach. She resisted blinking back at it.

Sister Lucia was on her hands and knees peering into all the eggs on the top layer. Sister Faustina wondered if she included these yet-brainless hatchlings in her evening prayers. Probably. Such a sweet one. It was a wonder she had the spine to do what they were doing.

"So—the priest."

"I've kept him away from the Reverend Mother." Sister Lucia prodded one of the spheres and watched as the color flushed and then evened again. "He doesn't know signing. He might get it into his head to learn, though. This is not sustainable."

On his first evening on the ship, Father Giovanni had clambered up on one of their dining chairs and taken the old crucifix off the chapel wall. He'd brought out a new one from the plethora of bags that Sister Faustina had dragged on board for him. They'd stood beneath him as he hung it, and then stood in silence when he turned around and showed it off like a proud father showing off a new infant.

"It's a bit graphic, isn't it?" asked Sister Ewostatewos. The crucifix had Jesus's face twisted in a rictus of pain, his limbs twisting against the nails, the torn flesh dripping red-painted blood down the cross. Compared to their old crucifix, with the smushed-face, cartoonish Son of God on his balsa wood cross, it was disturbing. Sister Faustina had stared into the darkness painted inside Jesus's open mouth and heard him screaming. "I mean . . . it doesn't really exemplify an air of peaceful contemplation, does it?"

"Our Lord suffered for us," the priest said, from above them on the chair. With his long legs, his head scraped the chapel roof, and the mossy fronds tickled at his hair. He batted them away. "It is only right that we remember that, and seek to be worthy of that pain."

It had not endeared him to any of them, aside from Sister Mary Catherine, who was so overjoyed to have an Earth-trained priest on board that she followed him around like a tracking drone. His other changes did not sit well either—the daily logs he kept and transmitted back to Earth, the demand that they hand out gospel tracts on humanitarian missions, or the way he spoke of Earth Central Governance with a reverence that approached that which he had for the Vatican.

"You could poison him," Sister Faustina said. Sister Lucia's head shot up. "I'm kidding, of course." She would say an extra Hail Mary tonight. She was losing her grip on piety, because of him. She had always had to work at it.

"She will get worse," Sister Lucia said. "Her nightmares already are. She's scared, though she'd never say it. And if she passes, or if he discovers what's happening and insists she retire back to the first system . . ."

"His authority will be unchallenged." So far the priest and the Reverend Mother had kept a kind of truce, only acting if they were unanimous. It was a fragile truce, held together only by the assumption that they held equal power on the ship, that the Reverend Mother could not challenge Father Giovanni's authority and he could not challenge hers. "He'll do whatever orders from Earth tell him to."

Father Giovanni was an actual Italian from actual Rome, and he believed in every word from the newly ascended pope with the dewy-eyed certainty of someone who had only left the seminary months before. This trip, apparently, was his first time leaving the safe embrace of gravity and he managed to mention this at least once an hour. Most often more. Many of the adjustments to spaceborn life he found primitive, upsetting, and uncomfortable. They had not shut off the gravity since he arrived, not even on holy days, because it upset his stomach. He was very well-meaning, and like most people who were well-meaning and ignorant, he bulldozed through everything in his way with not even a thought.

"Look at this." Sister Lucia brought a hymnal out of her bag, one of the new ones that Father Giovanni had brought with him from Earth. So far Sister Faustina hadn't found so many differences between it and the decades-old ones they had been using. Just a few stylistic grammar changes and some updated instrumentation because no one, out here, was going to be playing a pipe organ. Sister Lucia lifted the book to the light glowing off the eggs and carefully worked her thumbnail under the endpapers so that the thin page came free of the cardboard cover. When she held it close enough, a watermark appeared in the bottom left corner.

Sister Faustina leaned in to see it. A globe, two hands embracing around it. "Is that . . . ?"

"Earth Central Governance. They paid for them, apparently. I asked the father about it. He said, and I quote, 'They have taken quite seriously to acts of holy charity.' *Holy charity.* As if it's charity to indebt one of the largest religions in the four systems to you."

"Not only that. Back in the old days, before the war, everyone who wanted land on a habitable planet had to get their charters through ECG, did you know that? They had to list everyone going with them, everyone they were taking, and exactly where they would land. You were obligated to report back once a year what you were producing and how, and if you didn't, the jackboots might show up to repossess the colony and drag you back to Earth. Once upon a time, Central Governance had a map of everyone in the systems, and every place worth owning or worth destroying. They can't get that back—it would be impossible—but they can track where these books are going, where we are distributing them, how many more we need to order."

"They can start mapping the systems again, based on distribution. We'll be helping them track everyone we meet. You only need a map—"

"—if you want to own a place."

Sister Faustina did not suggest again out loud that it might be better if they just killed the priest and feigned ignorance, but she would have to say another set of prayers in penance tonight.

~

The Reverend Mother knew exactly what was happening. Faustina and Lucia, she knew, had come to think of her as a doddering old woman, barely able to hold the unraveling tapestry of her thoughts in her head. The priest thought she was a spaceborn nobody, a provincial Mother Superior so happy to bend to her Earthly betters who were much closer to the mouth of the Church. They were both right. At this point she had lived more of her life on a ship than on soil, and she was happy to let men far away study the finer details of theology for her. And she *was* losing her mind. As she tried to gather up the threads of her thoughts they only snarled and tangled in her hands. She was not what she had been. Reality escaped her more often than not, images from the past dancing across the visions of today. She woke from her dreams convinced the bombs were falling again, convinced again it was her fault.

And it had been her fault, in part. She had been in the room where they chose the end of the world-that-was. She had not dropped the bombs but she had asked those young, idealistic men and women drafted straight out of the schools to drop them. It had started so innocently. Her husband was an army scientist, a politician, a rising star in Earth Central Governance. The other colonies and the far-flung asteroid belts were growing restless. Entertainment was hard to get in those days. It was hard to transmit anything across channels not owned by ECG, and ECG didn't want to waste their precious bandwidth on TV shows and dramas. She had come up with the idea for Radio Terra, and then she had become its voice. It was just small broadcasts at first—the news from the biggest outposts, little stories submitted by lower-level government officials with morals that subtly encouraged cooperation with central authorities.

She had always been told she had a beautiful voice, a voice like honey and milk and hot smoky whiskey, a voice to bring men and women to their knees. With Earth Central Governance's relays at her disposal, her voice was the clearest sound in the cosmos, the only recording that came through to ships in the third system and sad, desolate little mining colonies that couldn't afford entertainment subscriptions. Her voice tumbled through the stars, automatically downloading into any comms array that ran off ECG technology, whispering *Earth is the mother of all of humanity and she loves you.* Whispering *No one will ever care for you like Earth does and you will die horribly in the vacuum without her charity.* Whispering, *Any man among you who speaks of independence is a traitor.*

Interspersed with the outright propaganda were audio dramas with better production value than anything else on the radio waves. That was the real draw. Everyone tuned in for the dramas. They ran day and night from Earth and didn't have to be listened to in chronological order so anyone, anywhere, could listen. Some episodes Radio Terra broadcast only for a short time, so that ships would have to trade each other the recordings. Some of those limited-run casts were more valuable than refined chromium.

Wars were fought in hearts and minds as much as they were fought in blood and bullets. She had turned what might have been one quick war into three solar systems of civil wars, each asteroid and planet and moon turning against itself before it finally turned against Earth.

She hadn't even realized a war had started for so long.

It began with a whisper, not a bang. A nothing colony on an iridium-mining asteroid stormed an ECG inspection ship that tried to land, hauled out the inspectors and the soldiers, and pulled their helmets off so they burned in the unfiltered radiation from the sun and suffocated. Earth retaliated by blowing the asteroid up underneath the miners, so that those who survived the depressurization were forced to scatter. The news didn't even filter back to Earth for a month, and it seemed like so much nothing—how many times had these small rebellions risen up, how many times had they crushed them like ants under a boot? Then Mars seeded their orbit with mines. Then the ECG troops on the Moon declared martial law to keep control of their closest colony. Then they started receiving messages from ships—their last messages, the dying cries of Central Governance marine carriers locked in battles with mining transports and rickety little orbital stations that should never have stood a chance. They didn't when they were alone, of course. But they finally hated ECG enough to overcome their differences.

She had gone on the radio that night and pleaded with all the red-blooded, good-hearted children of Earth to put an end to this foolishness. She said they could not survive without Earth. They would not be human without Earth. And god help her, so many of them believed her. It was so very, very bloody, what happened next.

She saw their ghosts now, in the ship. She'd never been on a living ship before taking her vows. There should be no ghosts here. But they haunted the pale shadows between bioluminescent lamps and the softly curving corners of halls made from muscle and moss. When she knelt in prayer she heard a mother scream as her son turned on her with a rifle. She saw battle lines drawn in the sand of desert worlds, the great glass spheres of atmosphere on airless moons cracking.

Sister Lucia, bless her, was sequencing her DNA to explain what was going wrong inside her head. Gene therapy had come so far, the girl said. Many types of dementia were completely curable, she said. She had such determination. The Reverend Mother knew better. This was not just an accident of genetics, a decaying strand of DNA that had twisted her memories against her. This was holy judgment.

"You're awfully quiet, Mother," said Father Giovanni. She had, frankly, forgotten he was sitting next to her. He took her look for offense and jumped. "I mean . . . lost in thought. Not quiet, of course."

They were plotting a new course for the ship together. He had determined that there was a sector of this system that had never been given the Good Word, and he was intent on having the *Our Lady of Impossible Constellations* be the first to bring it to them. The Reverend Mother considered proselytizing to be the least interesting of their duties. Sister Faustina had picked up a request for medical assistance coming from a distant ringed planet, and though it was farther, she would rather have them attend to the needy.

The priest huffed through his nose when she wrote this to him. "You've read our new directives. His Holiness has decreed that spreading the Good Word of the Lord is the highest duty of women in the religious life. And I have all those Bibles that we should give out to those in need of them! Surely it would be better, as a practical consideration, to reduce the weight on the ship?"

Peach fuzz smoothed the lines of his upper lip. She simply did not have the energy to debate theology with him. She wrote, *I will consider it. If you will excuse me, Sister Faustina asked I meet her in the communications room.*

A lie, but the communications room was quiet and small, and she was hearing the rattling phantom of automatic fire *tatt-tatt-tatt-tatt* echoing far away in her hearing. It was hard to concentrate on his insipid, nattering voice when she could hear men dying all around. He let her go, with a smile that said he had won.

Sister Faustina jumped from her chair when the Reverend Mother entered the communications room.

"Please, have a seat."

The Reverend Mother shook her head. She was not so fragile yet that she couldn't keep her feet. Soon, she knew, that would not be true. She looked at the screen, where Sister Faustina was filtering out incoming transmissions, peeling the worthless chatter away. She saw, overlaid on it, the WANTED poster with her husband's face and President Shen's and the dark silhouette that was supposed to be her. Her husband was long dead, she knew. She had seen him in the early stages of ringeye, though she'd stopped loving him by then. She had seen the rebels who'd stormed Paris execute Shen, but in the smoke and rubble afterward his body was lost, and so rumors still swirled that he had pulled a last great escape. He never would have lain low, though. She was the last of them left alive. She tried to concentrate through the poster.

Sister Faustina laughed uncomfortably, like she'd been caught listening to a risqué romantic audiodrama. "Silly, isn't it? I'm shocked they still send these things around. I'm not even sure who we would turn in a fugitive to. Though I've heard that Earth is still using the Radio Terra recordings. They come through the array sometimes."

The Reverend Mother gripped the back of the chair and let the shudder roll through her, skin to flesh to bone, and stopped it before it showed.

"Mother," Sister Faustina said, and her voice was gentle in a way that Faustina so rarely was. This was love, wasn't it? For a woman who was so fundamentally uncomfortable with gentleness to try and be gentle with you? What a life she had built here, and she had never deserved it. "What is it? Are you here with us?"

"I have come to make a request of you," she signed. She had not realized she was going to ask this until this moment.

"Of course." Again Faustina gestured to the seat, and the Reverend Mother shook her head.

"Before I lose myself completely, I want to make confession. To you."

Sister Faustina did not flinch, just as the Reverend Mother had known she would not.

She could have objected. She could have pointed out that confession was one of those duties held so sacred that only priests could truly perform it. She could have said that it was too great a burden, and the Reverend Mother had no right to ask her to take on the weight of her own heavy heart. And she would have been right.

Instead, Sister Faustina met her eyes steadily. She closed the messages open on the comms screen so that there was nothing distracting them from this conversation.

"Why me?" she asked. "Why not Lucia?"

"Lucia believes so much in me," the Reverend Mother

signed.

"And I've already got enough secrets, I can carry yours too? Is that it?"

She shrugged.

Sister Faustina tipped her head back, looking up at the ceiling like this was a chapel and she was asking for the Lord's help, like she was a Mars-drama interpretation of a religious sister, always looking at the sky like God was actually a bearded man sitting in the clouds. Her nostrils flared when she breathed out. "You've done something really bad, haven't you."

"Yes," the Reverend Mother signed. "But it isn't time to tell you yet."

A muscle in the corner of Sister Faustina's mouth twitched like there was something she wanted to say to that. But then a bell on the communications array started ringing, and Sister Faustina started forward to hook her headphones back over her ears. The Reverend Mother jumped too. She hadn't heard that bell for years. Someone was sending a distress signal straight to them. Not out into general space, like a beacon would. Straight to their array.

Sister Faustina leaned over the array, one hand pressing the speaker to her ear, the other gripping a knob on the control panel, adjusting the audio for the distortion of space. Her knuckles were white, the nailbeds pink where she gripped the controls.

The Reverend Mother grabbed her shoulder and Sister Faustina tore her attention away like she had forgotten she was there.

"The colony," she said. "Terret's moon." She let go of the audio controls and pressed the back of her hand over her mouth, which scared the Reverend Mother more than any alarm bell could. Sister Faustina did not scare and never shocked.

Sister Lucia crept around and picked up the second headset and held it to her ear. No one but the ship breathed. "They're infected with ringeye."

III.

Sic transit gloria mundi

GEMMA LAY UNDER ONE of the hydroponic plant beds, where the air circulated the moisture rising off the water, cooling her face. It almost felt like being in a forest, with the sounds of the leaves rustling in the climate control system's breeze and the nutrient-rich water pumping over the vegetables' roots.

Vauca laughed. "Is that what a forest is like? I've never been." She turned over onto her side and bumped her head on one of the crocks fermenting cabbage into kimchi and garlicky sauerkraut. There was a leak in one of the feeder lines and after forty-five minutes in the cool damp they'd finally replaced the tubing. Not that they were rushing.

"Sort of." Gemma searched for a way to describe the feeling of so many trees. She had only been in forests a few times herself, and years ago. "It's like . . . there are so many lives. They talk to each other through their roots, you know. They send information back and forth in patterns of nutrients and bioelectricity."

"Like the shiplings! Well, maybe."

"I bet we could inject one of the shiplings with magnetic dye and watch how it travels through the others." Gemma let a curl of Vauca's hair wrap around her fingers and slip through. She was not so young anymore, not really. On the station where she had grown up, she would be married with three children in the creche by now. But she felt like a blushing, budding teenager, waiting for someone to ask her to dance at an eclipse festival, wondering what it would feel like to have someone else's skin touch her neck, her cheek, the curve of her back. Vauca's hair smelled like vanilla. How very strange their lives were, she thought, that their toiletries could smell like a spice she had never seen in real life, that would not grow beyond Earth.

"Interesting. How would we track it? We'd have to set up a CT scan net outside the ship and that would be extraordinarily large."

"Hmm." It was a problem. Would it be possible to do a CT scan in sections, with handheld scanners? Surely one of the shipyards had developed a more space-efficient diagnostic tool. Then again, ships produced such large egg clutches and so few were expected to grow to size, most of the time shipyards just disposed of problematic larvae.

The door to the hydroponics bay slid open and

Gemma jumped. She still wasn't used to the sounds of a metal ship, where doors slid and hissed instead of squelching and sucking.

"Gemma?" It was Jared, the comms officer. "There's a call for you."

Gemma shimmied out from under the table and Vauca followed after. "Who's calling me?" She couldn't think of a single person who would be. Not directly, in real time. It took a lot of power and bandwidth to send a targeted call and keep the channel open for responses.

"A woman named Lucia on your old ship."

Something was wrong. She ran for the comms room. Sister Lucia's face loomed in the screen and Sister Faustina stood behind her like a reaper. Sister Faustina's wimple was askew, a snaking coil of salt-and-pepper hair writhing down her shoulder.

"How much of our ringeye treatment do you have?" Sister Lucia asked, as soon as she made it in view of the camera.

She didn't understand. "I took a couple batches with me. I've been tinkering with it."

"Does it work?"

"I don't exactly have a live ringeye sample to test it!" No one would dare keep that on board a ship. The risks were unthinkable. She had tested her samples on less lethal cousins to ringeye, like the shadowpox that plagued the second system, with good results. But good results on an annoying rash didn't mean they would have good results on a deadly hemorrhagic fever. "What's happened?"

Please, God, don't let ringeye have broken out on the ship. She imagined Sister Ewostatewos, thin already, curled crumpled and crimped in her bed, her eyes black and orange striations like the rings of Saturn, blood bubbling from her mouth. She imagined the Reverend Mother in the clutches of fever, her elderly heart giving out after only a day. No one would be brave enough to render them aid. They would be quarantined while the disease burned through them. After they all died, the ship would be euthanized by whatever local government was unlucky enough to be closest, then burned. Gemma had never been on a ringeye quarantine zone. The Reverend Mother had, she knew, as part of the only teams willing to go into the zones, and when she spoke of it her hands went to her rosary without her meaning them to.

Only a few groups were even willing to go near disease-stricken colonies—some orders of nuns, a Buddhist order of physician-monks, a shipful of rabbis who had taken the disease on for their mission, a few secular cohorts of humanitarian scientists. Most of those people, she knew, had died in the same hospitals as those they had come to help.

"The Phoyongsa III colony," Sister Lucia said. Her face was drawn and still.

"Oh my God, that baby."

"Yes. So, we're going back. We'll rendezvous with you in a few hours and I'll take what stock you have."

"It won't be enough for all of them, even if it works." Thirty people. She thought of Terret's baby boy crying alone for a mother who was never going to come.

"Do we have what you would need to make more?"

Gemma looked up and found the crew of the *Cheng I Sao* assembled behind her. Vauca and Jared; Werrin, the captain for all that meant on a communal-property ship; Yevet, the cook.

"Did she say ringeye?" Werrin asked.

"There was a ringeye colony on a moon of the planet where I grew up. In school they took us to walk around the ruins and you could still see where the bloodstains were," Yevet said. Their mouth twisted at the memory.

"It will take more than a few hours to produce another batch," Gemma said. "A day at least. We would have to follow the *Our Lady of Impossible Constellations* halfway to the colony."

Vauca tilted her head against the edge of the door frame, her arms crossed over her chest. "You want to go with them, don't you?"

How did they already know each other so well?

Gemma saw every emotion in the crisscross of those arms: sadness, fear, strength. "Yes. I swore to myself I would still do good if I left the habit. And—I know these people. They welcomed us and I ate their food and blessed their marriages. I can't just leave and wish them well."

"You'll need more hands than a dozen nuns," said Werrin.

"I can't ask you to put yourselves in danger."

"And it *is* going to be dangerous!" Yevet said. They shuddered. "Gods below, do you really want to risk dying like that?"

"I have to."

"We should go," Vauca said.

Yevet scoffed. "You're saying that because you want to impress her."

"No." Vauca looked out the viewscreen, toward the cool, orange arm of Andromeda, millions of empty light-years away. "We should go because I would want someone to come for us. We're all just scattered, lonely specks out here, unless we try to be more. We shouldn't be brutal just because the universe is."

Yevet was quiet.

"Think of it as practicality," Jared said. "If we left Gemma, we would have to put up with Vauca moping until our flightpaths crossed again."

They put it to a vote, as a formality, because they voted on everything. It was unanimous. They were going to Phoyongsa III.

~

Sister Lucia held the vial aloft in front of her assembled sisters. The liquid inside was amber, viscous. She used to think it ridiculous when secular people told her that all nuns looked the same, but here, with all of them wearing the same tight, worried grimace, she understood. Unified in one purpose, they were a single weapon, the fingers of a single hand. By now the ship would be entering the gravity well of the mother-planet; they were only hours from Phoyongsa III and whatever awaited them there. "If this works, the victims should cease to be contagious twenty-four bells after the first dose. The virus can live airborne for longer than that, so keep your respirators on the whole time we're on the surface."

Sister Mary Catherine raised her hand, her fingers quivering. "How long can it live airborne?"

"We don't know."

They didn't have Level 4-certified biohazard suits—they weren't funded by any deep-pocketed civilian gov and they were not one of the orders whose sole mission was to follow the black foot of pandemic as it strode across the known systems, leaving footprints of phlegm and bile and blood in its wake. They would be wearing their vacsuit skins under their habits, and nitrile gloves that would not do anything more than make them feel a little secure. If this were the first system, where every half-decent rock was full of people, they could wait for one of the real authorities to arrive and render aid. But here, where the distances between settled places was so great people could sometimes go years without seeing a ship, there was no one.

"You will have to inject it into the jugular vein." Sister Lucia demonstrated with a used syringe. "Ringeye victims are known for their unnatural strength. They will fight you. You cannot allow any bodily fluids to come into contact with your skin. It's highly, highly contagious. We are here to render aid and bury the dead, not to become burdens ourselves."

A sound chimed overhead. Sister Faustina looked up, something like a mix of confusion and fear written in the lines of her face. Sister Lucia did not like it when Sister Faustina showed either of those emotions. It was usually a very bad sign. The other woman slipped away from the group and out the hatch. She returned only a moment later.

Sister Lucia was about to show how to remove a pair of gloves without getting any of the secretions on them onto your skin, but she stopped. "What was that alarm, Sister?"

"Proximity." Sister Faustina huffed. She must have run from the lab to the comms room and back. "Mother, Father Giovanni, there are four Central Governance ships in orbit around Phoyongsa III."

"What?" Sister Lucia said. Her hand loosened on the vial—she caught it just before she lost it completely. They could not waste any of this. She set it on her workbench snug in the case with the rest of them.

"There are. Four Central Governance ships. Outside Phoyongsa III. Did I *stutter*, Sister?" Sister Faustina bared her teeth, that scraped-down look of pure bridled anger she got when Central Governance came too close to them.

Sister Lucia drew herself up. "Excuse me."

Sister Faustina swallowed whatever hot rage she kept leashed inside herself and her face settled. "I'm sorry. Please excuse me. Father Giovanni, they have asked us to leave our present course and stay at least beyond Phoyongsa XI. They are saying they will not allow us to land on the moon."

All eyes turned to the priest. Father Giovanni was sweating, moisture gathering at the edge of his hairline. "Well. That's very unexpected. Did they give a good reason?"

"For our protection, of course." Sister Faustina's lips stretched thin, toward that animistic grimace again. "Please come speak with them. Perhaps you Earthers will understand each other better."

The Reverend Mother signed *Faustina!* over the priest's head, but he did not, apparently, pick up on her tone. They all followed him and crowded into the hatchway of the comms room, pressing their hands into the ship's muscles to keep it open so they could see the screen.

The man on the screen was rosy-cheeked, wearing a silver and gray uniform that struck Sister Lucia like something out of one of the cheaply made educational vids about the war she had been made to watch in school. He looked middle-aged, though rumor was the Earthers were hoarding a secret way to live centuries instead of decades, so who knew really. He certainly held himself like he expected nothing but respect and obedience. When the lag time between their ships caught up, she saw his upper lip twitch, like he was repressing a sneer, and she understood why Sister Faustina had such a gut-level reaction to Earthers like this.

"Part of the duty of the sisters' order is to care for the sick and dying, to offer them respite and kindness," Father Giovanni said. When he was talking to the soldier, he smoothed his voice into a radio-drama Earther accent, all the hard stops softened and the vowels drawn out long like hot taffy. "We merely wish to go to the surface to offer what comfort we can to these poor souls. And one of the sisters is a doctor. She believes she may have discovered a treatment for this awful disease, using the genes of our own ship. Perhaps it will ease their suffering, at least. Those people down there need not die alone."

Sister Lucia bristled at his phrasing, like she was a dilettante playing with vaccines. Better to close her mouth around that before she said something to escalate the situation. "There's a baby down there. We need to at least rescue him."

Not a spark of sympathy appeared on the lieutenant's face. "No one is going down to the surface. We have quarantined the moon. I will not see us spark a plague like during the war."

"There hasn't been a plague like that *since* the war," Sister Faustina said, leaning over Father Giovanni so she could glare right at the soldier. "And what authority do you have to stop us? We don't abide by Central Governance laws. This isn't the first system."

The soldier sighed deeply, picked a tablet up from in front of him, and sent something to their ship. The comms array pinged when the datapack downloaded. "These colonists signed a contract when they accepted the supplies from ECG's New Worlds Foundation. That contract entitled us to take over military duties on their colony in the event of—and I quote—a natural disaster or conflict that significantly threatened the rest of our signees, member colonies, and ships. An outbreak of ringeye more than qualifies. We will close orbit for eight weeks. If you want to stick around that long, we will allow you down afterward."

"There will be nothing but bodies," Sister Lucia said. "The *baby*."

"It is very unfortunate, yes."

"Unfortunate is not the word that comes to mind."

The soldier shrugged. "Do not attempt to travel closer to the moon. We will disable your ship. And I know those slugs don't move fast enough to evade us. And if you continue to resist our directive, we will board you and hold you until we are sure the danger period has passed."

"You certainly don't have the authority to do that," Sister Faustina said.

"Sister, I'm a good Catholic boy. I went to parochial school, I still can't wear collarless shirts. I do not want to do anything to inconvenience you. But listen to me carefully—no one owns this sad little corner of space. We have the power to enforce our authority."

The screen went dark. Father Giovanni sat back in the comms chair and yanked at his collar. "Well. Should we continue on our previous route? I have identified several colonies and mining camps that have not yet been visited—in their entire existence!—by representatives of the Church. And that request for medical assistance you received earlier—I suppose it would be on our way to stop there."

Silence fell as the sisters tried to think of a way to disagree with him without taking the Lord's name in vain.

"We are not leaving," said Sister Ewostatewos, surprising them all. She was so quiet, usually. But she also had the firm conviction of an iron rod. "Those people are part of our flock. We married them and blessed their child and their home. We have a duty."

"We can hardly resist three warships," the priest replied. "I don't see how it is a good use of our limited resources to continue to fight them."

"There are ways." Sister Lucia drummed her fingers on the comms board, thinking. "Gemma's ship might have an engine capable of tight maneuvers. I don't think they're in range of the ECG ships yet. We would have the element of surprise."

"I will not allow it." Father Giovanni stood up. Sister Lucia didn't think he meant to intimidate her, but he towered over her, and his hands were fists and it made every instinct in her snarl like a wild dog. "Those people are not our enemies. I know that is a very strange notion out here, where you all seem to hold these prewar fantasies that it's you against Earth, but the New Worlds Foundation does good work. They did good work for those people dying down there. And they are trying to do a good thing now by preventing that hideous disease from slaughtering millions again. It is painful, yes, but the greater good—"

"Have you forgotten Matthew?" Sister Faustina asked, and there was a dangerous tone in her voice, a tone that forgot their roles. "'And proclaim as you go, saying, "The kingdom of heaven is at hand." Heal the sick, raise the dead, cleanse lepers, cast out demons. You received without paying; give without pay.'"

He turned on her, and even she stepped back. "I will not have you cherry-pick theology at me. Do you think I have not noticed that you are the least faithful of these good women, skirting your obligations, doing only the devotion that is necessary? Do not pretend that you know more of His word than I do. The Bible also says *Render onto Caesar that which is Caesar's.* And this matter—quarantine, war—that is Caesar's."

He shouldered past them, through the hatch, away. Like he thought that was the end of it.

~

The *Cheng I Sao* hung behind a tiny moon—just a large

asteroid caught in an improbable orbit, really—while they waited for the Central Governance ship to turn away. They heard the entire exchange. Someone—Lucia or Faustina, Gemma wasn't sure—had opened a channel to them.

Vauca made a face. "What the fuck. Are priests supposed to be *pro*-Caesar?"

"That's not really what he meant—" Gemma began, and then waved it away. "Never mind. We can have a deep discussion of theology later, if you want. But look—there are shuttles on the surface."

The *Cheng I Sao* had been a long-range mining and geological survey ship, before Werrin bought it for two barrels of copper chit in a war-surplus junkyard. The interior was not much to look at, but the scanners on the ship were incredible. Far more powerful than the *Our Lady of Impossible Constellations* was equipped with. Which was probably why they were buying the lie that the Central Governance soldiers were merely holding quarantine. But Gemma could see at least three short-range shuttles, docked meters from the orange-tarp roofs and prefab houses of the colony. Three shuttles meant a dozen soldiers, at least. If they didn't want humanitarian nuns with a potential cure on the surface, why would they go themselves? Surely Navy transport ships didn't carry a full complement of biohazard suits.

A dozen armed soldiers, from Earth. What were they even doing in this *sector*, near this nothing-moon that hadn't even had a colony on it weeks ago, and close enough to be the first ones to respond to a distress call?

"Oh," she said, and it came out a gasp because her throat was closing on her. "Oh. Oh."

Vauca gripped her shoulder. She didn't know what was wrong but she felt the change of air in the room, like one of their portholes had cracked and that great gnawing cold outside was rushing through the fracture. "What?"

"The mandatory vaccines. Sister Lucia said they looked like injection sites from the mass-dose vaccines of the war. But you don't need that many vaccinations for an untouched, pre-scouted planet, do you? So what else did Central Governance put in those injections?" She leapt to her feet and knocked her tablet off the table. It clattered across the floor, denting the plastic screen. She didn't care. Her knees were trembling. This great, awful, horrific idea had rooted in her head and she could not shake it free. It kept unfurling in her mind, like Eden's serpent, its fangs waiting to sink into flesh. "How long does it take to get here from the first system, anyway? Two jumps plus another couple weeks of traveling through the system? That puts us solidly within the incubation window."

"Gemma," Vauca said. She was leaning over Gemma's

now-vacated chair, her fingers digging into the foam padding. She feared Central Governance as much as anyone out here did. "I don't understand."

"Say you're Central Governance. You believe all these people, all these planets with their minerals and water and agricultural space, should belong to you. You ruled the universe once, of course. So you start growing again. You start funding religious missionaries and sending propaganda with colonists. You start rebuilding your communications relays and your supply lines, because people will trust you if you give them infrastructure, right? All roads led to Rome, remember, because the Romans knew that you must be the center of the world to rule it. But that's too slow. That's a plan of generations. Centuries, not decades. In the minds of everyone else in the universe, you are the great destroyer. But meanwhile, your oceans are rising, your continents are packed with people, your resources depleted from years of poor management. Swaths of your planet are irradiated still. You have to feed all these people, so you have to buy food at a premium from those colonies who you used to own."

It was dawning on Vauca. She shivered. "If there was a plague . . ."

"If there was a plague, everyone would need the planet with the universities and the many legions of doctors to save them. They would need coordination. Centralization. Who controls the communications relays? Who controls the largest organized military in the four systems?"

"You think they infected those people with ringeye deliberately, knowing they were going to an isolated sector where the outbreak would be easy to control."

"More than that. The disease only thrives in a live host. It's almost impossible to grow it in animals, or in a laboratory. People have tried. It's part of why it's so hard to create a treatment. I think they infected these people because no one would hear their distress in time to investigate, and they are using them to grow more doses of it. If you just needed the report to spread, to cause panic, you would not send all your men to the surface. You only go to the surface if you need to bring something back."

"Because one colony will not be enough."

No. She could imagine what the next targets would be. Orion's Daughter, a small, warm planet in the second system, the only world with medical schools to rival Earth's. The cluster of terraformed moons around Argos in the third system, which had come together into a republic and kept a standing military—a rarity, beyond the first system. Most worlds relied on militias or vague common-defense pacts, if they considered such impossibilities as another system-wide war at all. A disease with no known cure, rampaging through the richest of the independent worlds. Where would everyone else have to turn? How attractive would the promises of Central Governance look then?

~

The Reverend Mother felt something disintegrate inside her as Gemma explained. It was horrific. It was disgusting. And it was born of the horrific, disgusting things that she herself had done those decades ago. She had thought the war was over, but it was not and never would be. Its atrocities kept giving birth to more and more and more. Those soldiers carrying out their duties on the surface were her children as much as any she might have borne. Without her, they would not have been born into this world, would not have been set on this path, would not have come here to this moon to allow these innocent people to die.

"We are going to the surface," she signed. "We are going to rescue Terret and her colony."

"Mother," Sister Faustina said, and laid a hand gently on her arm. Gentleness did not become her. It looked awkward on her. "We can't possibly get past their ships. We want to save the colony too, but I don't know how."

She looked at all of them assembled here, Faustina and Lucia and Ewostatewos and Varvara and the others, even

Mary Catherine, who had come around in the end. She loved them all so much. She had learned, on this ship, how to love people without wanting anything back from them. Without loving them because of what they could give her. She had not even loved her husband like that, God rest his soul.

"We will transfer everyone to Gemma's ship," she signed. "The *Cheng I Sao* is fast enough for evasive maneuvers, assuming they have a pilot worth his salt. We shall put Father Giovanni into the emergency pod and send him off if he refuses. Someone will be along to pick him up soon enough."

"They will be watching us," Sister Lucia said.

"Someone will remain on board to maintain the appearance that the ship is still inhabited." And then, right as she signed it, she saw the truth of this open up before her. So this was why God had brought her to this ship, and this moon, at this time. She was meant to be here. She could never make amends for all the things she had done in the life before this one, but she could make one small reparation. "I will stay. It will be fine. They are most likely to treat me with deference, anyway."

"Mother." Sister Lucia's eyes crinkled the way they did when she got upset that life provided no easy answers. Poor child—it must be so hard to live with a heart as soft as hers. "What if—what if you feel—" She cut off, struggling to find an appropriate euphemism.

"Don't worry. I'm sure the Lord will protect me, and all of us."

Sister Lucia did not seem convinced, but there was no other way. They had only hours. Sister Faustina brought the ship around the barren little half-moon the *Cheng I Sao* was hiding behind. The Central Governance soldiers seemed happy to let them go, but everyone watched from the portholes in case they changed their minds. So lucky, they were, that Father Giovanni in his hubris had downplayed Sister Lucia and Gemma's discovery. The Reverend Mother had a dark feeling that they would not have been allowed to depart if he had framed their treatment as more than the fanciful hobby of two uneducated, backwater religious sisters.

They sent a message to the soldiers that they were going to sit on the surface of the barren moon for a little while to rest the ship and plan their flight path. The lieutenant sent back an uninterested *Noted.* They found the crevice where the *Cheng I Sao* was sitting on the surface next to a crumbling rock face where it was indistinguishable from the boulders scattering the surface. There was nowhere level enough for their ships to extend pressurized boarding ramps. Everyone got into their vacsuits and skins and stickboots.

Father Giovanni emerged from his room just as the

last of the sisters had closed the seam on her vacsuit skin. The Reverend Mother came with them, to bless them on their way, and she drew herself up to her full height. He took in the scene as well as—for the first time apparently, oh what sweet Earther senses he had still to lose—the fact that they were no longer moving.

"I did not agree to this," he said.

"You don't have to," said Sister Lucia.

"You have obligations to your convent duties. It is part of your vows. As is obedience. There is no rebellion in this life, Sisters." His face was mottled red, and his right hand was clenched against the chain that led from his belt to his gilded liturgical, like he could feel his grip on them slipping. "I have already given you direction. Please. I will call those soldiers out there to stop you. I do not want you all to die, believe me, this is for your own good."

"Let us do what we know to be right," Sister Lucia said. "If we die, we will know we died doing good works, and that is all any of us have asked of this life."

He coughed a laugh and turned from them to go to the hatch. The Revered Mother reached for him—to do what, she didn't know—but Sister Lucia closed the hatch between them. Through the muscle wall she heard his thundering steps headed toward the comms room. Then the footsteps faltered. And went silent. Sister Lucia had closed her eyes and was counting softly under her breath.

"What was that?" Sister Ewostatewos asked. Sister Lucia opened her eyes, took a deep breath, and reopened the hatch. Father Giovanni lay prone in the hall, feet from the comms room, completely still. "Is he—? Goodness, Sister."

Sister Lucia shook her head. "I vented some of our nitrogen reserves into the hall. It's the same weight as oxygen—he didn't feel a thing. But he'll wake up soon."

They got the priest into the escape pod and sealed it up, but did not launch it. "Perhaps he will come to his senses," said Sister Varvara, while trembling inside her climate-controlled suit. Unlikely, the Reverend Mother thought. She made sure to find the launch button on the navigation panel before anything. The hatch squelched closed behind the other sisters, mucus filling the small fissures between the bands of muscle to seal it completely. The Reverend Mother stood on the other side, in the air, watching them one by one step from the warm embrace of the ship to the cold dust of the surface of the asteroid, leaving footprints that would endure far beyond their mortal bodies, until someone else came and swept them away or it all fell into the sun.

~

Gemma's crew were a motley bunch, Sister Lucia thought, as the all crowded together into the *Cheng I Sao*'s nav room. How appropriate. The engineer who had stolen her away was a handsome woman, with hands that looked like they could do hard work. Gemma was being more circumspect with them around than Sister Lucia thought she normally would be, but when the pilot lifted them off the surface of the rock she reached out and held one of those strong hands in her own.

They skimmed along the gravity of the asteroid-moon. The pilot sent them wobbling across the circumference like so much debris. The *Our Lady of Impossible Constellations* grew smaller and smaller and disappeared from view.

"She'll be all right," Sister Faustina said, for Lucia's ears alone, but it sounded like a platitude.

"There they are," said Vauca, the engineer. She was leaning over one of the screens. Three red dots showed the ECG ships standing guard over the colony.

The pilot swallowed, his Adam's apple moving thickly under the skin. "I'm going to put us on the right trajectory and then turn off the thrusters—hopefully we'll drift close before they notice us."

The ship shuddered as the engines fired, and then, right as they crested a ridge on the moon and broke gravity, he turned them off. The ship went silent. It was so much quieter than a living ship. No wonder they were called deadships. No gurgle of digestion, no shudders from muscles twitching, no ghost of a heartbeat overhead. Only the thin hum of the life support systems sucking in carbon dioxide and hissing out oxygen, and that was just the faint suggestion of a sound at the very edges of her hearing. Everyone held their breath. From the porthole, Sister Lucia saw one of the military ships as they sailed past. Far enough away to look insignificant, close enough to fire on and destroy them. The pilot bit into his thumbnail again and again until she saw a thin crescent of blood well under the broken nail. She had the absurd urge to open her case and count the vials there, as if that would help anything.

The colony came into view—the green continent and the regular brown squares where the earth had been tilled. They were not close enough yet to see the houses, but there was the patch of green where they sat.

"Almost," said the pilot. They sailed past the second ship, which was just a dark glimmer in space, its cannons like two silver needles.

The radio crackled. They all stared at it.

"Approaching vessel, this is Lieutenant Richardson of the Fifth Naval Division, Earth Central Governance. We have established a quarantine zone around this moon. Turn back."

"I thought you turned off our communications?" the captain said.

"They overrode it," the pilot replied. This was, Sister Lucia remembered, an Earth-made vessel. The pilot's hand hovered uselessly over the button to respond. "What should I do?" Already, the first ship was turning on them.

The captain hit the button on the array. "Greetings, Lieutenant. I am the captain of this vessel. We have been contracted to deliver seeds to this moon. Will you be paying the balance on our contract? We are owed quite a bit of chit from these colonists. Please respond." He gestured at the pilot, who fired the thrusters.

"Turn back, or we will fire on you," the lieutenant replied. Over the terrible radio he sounded alien, mechanical. "You can submit a request for reimbursement to the Central Governance outpost in this system after the end of the quarantine. Also, we are not receiving your identification signature. Please identify yourselves."

The pilot increased their speed. The ship rumbled. The military vessel outside had come to face them.

"Vessel, you are increasing your speed. We will fire upon you. This is a final warning."

"Shit," the pilot said. "The one in front of us is coming around too. We're not *that* fast, Captain."

The captain hesitated, and Sister Lucia saw him weighing whether to break off or not. But they were too far into it for that.

Then, just as Sister Lucia was wondering how it would feel to be sucked out into space, the *Our Lady of Impossible Constellations* rose from behind the moon.

Their radio crackled again. They heard a woman clearing her throat. Sister Faustina frowned.

"Hello, out there, to anyone listening in on this fine evening. Specifically you, Lieutenant Richardson." Yes, that was a woman. And it sounded so *familiar.* That greeting was ingrained somewhere deep in the recesses of Sister Lucia's mind. A sound half-remembered from childhood, like the cadence of a favorite lullaby. What *was* it? "This is Mrs. August, of Radio Terra, and I *outrank* you."

Sister Lucia did not understand. The voice of Radio Terra? That woman was—that woman should be—long dead. No one had seen her for decades. How could she have possibly hidden for all these years, when her voice was the most well-known in all the four systems? How could she have said a word without being discovered and turned over to any one of the dozens of polities that would have liked her head? Even Earth, which still worshipped her like a goddess, would not have been safe. And then it dawned on her, and she felt the solid ground of years shift and crack under her feet.

Sister Faustina barked a laugh. "I guess she really did

have something to confess."

~

The Reverend Mother had known there was a reason she had lived. Lived through the war, and the rebellion on Earth, and the crushing of it. Lived through plagues and wars and traveling in a small, squishy body for years through unforgiving space. This was why. She knew it as soon as she opened her mouth and found that her tongue still worked as it should even after this long disuse.

Silence reigned on the radio. She watched the *Cheng I Sao* inch closer to the moon, forgotten for the moment. That wouldn't last long. She had bought only minutes.

The lieutenant opened the channel again, and she heard a shiver in his voice. She wondered what they taught about her in Earth schools now. Was she a hero, or a monster? Either way, he must feel he was standing in the presence of a legend.

"Please explain," he said, simply. What a question.

She settled for: "Let this ship pass. My authorization code is being transmitted now." She sent it through the radio waves. Back before the war, she could ask anything of any ECG entity at all, be it soldier or diplomat or low-level lackey, with this code. She heard the soldiers muttering.

"This—" The lieutenant broke off. "Mrs. August. This is your code, but this is not from our current standards."

She could feel the gears in his mind turning, but the *Cheng I Sao* was not close enough yet. She had to buy them enough time to break the atmosphere. After that, they would be on their own.

"Are you questioning my identity?" she asked sweetly. She had a voice, soft and kind, that she had used for reading children's bedtime stories into the transmitter. She gambled that this man had been raised on those stories. On her reading tales of great valor for the defense of Earth. "Surely your ship is equipped with the audio equipment necessary to confirm that I am who I claim to be, and not an impostor or a reconstruction. I don't understand why you are being so resistant. This is a very simple matter."

She heard him swallow, a great gulp of air. Soon enough he would dig into the restricted files every military ship carried and confirm that she had not been hidden in some bunker on the moon for these forty years, that she was not a great secret agent of Central Governance, and that everyone with any power on Earth assumed her dead. He would be angry, she was sure. You always were when you learned something ugly about the world.

The *Cheng I Sao* broke the clouds on the moon. The

Reverend Mother let herself relax, just for a moment. The ghosts in the edges of her eyes swam forward, laying over this ship the image of another. She saw not the green fuzz of a living ship's symbiotic moss, but the cold steel of a prewar strategy room. The viewscreen showing the ECG military cruisers outside became a pane of treated glass, looking out over gray rock and habitat bubbles and, far away, the innocent blue of the Earth and her oceans. This was where she had last seen the war. She looked to her right. There he was, just where she knew he would be, in his white lab coat. He hadn't been wearing a lab coat that day, she knew that in the logical part of herself, but she had so rarely seen him without it that it seemed correct for him to be wearing it now, as a phantom.

She wanted to say hello to him, but she was forced to live out history once more, and her mouth stayed stubbornly silent. In those last brutal days, she had found herself growing more and more silent, as if having used her tongue to do evil she could no longer use it for anything else.

"Do you think," her husband said, "that anyone will remember us fondly? History is written by the victors, after all. Even if the victors are a bunch of scrabbling, squabbling children who will not know what a good thing they've destroyed."

It was this moment, she remembered, when she had

felt her love for him wither and die. Only moments before, California had slid into the sea. They had watched Shen, who had been a friend to them both before he became a monster, beheaded in the ruins of the city where they had fallen in love and spent so much of their lives. She did not care if they were remembered fondly, or at all.

"I've set it loose," he said.

He turned to her and his eyes were ringed pink and orange and gray. In reality he had only started showing symptoms. She knew what he was talking about. He had called it their child. He had called it their swift and terrible sword. Their virus, a destroyer of worlds. Almost certainly lethal. Highly contagious. Later, the reports would say: *It's as if someone made this, how could evolution create something so cruel?* And no one would ever know that they were right, that ringeye had been the last vindictive act of an angry man, who could not lose without taking as many with him as possible. And she was just as bad, for she had lied to herself about what he was doing. Disease was natural, she had thought, in her ignorance and her callousness. This would not make a difference.

The only reason she had survived was because she had run from him. She hadn't meant to flee. She'd gotten on a supplier ship with every intention of coming back when the roiling disgust inside her had settled back where it belonged. But the next morning, the Martians took the Moon. Half the habitats depressurized in the fighting, including her home.

"Mrs. August," the lieutenant said. She snapped back into herself. The images of yesterday faded to the background but did not dissipate. "Why are you on board a convent ship? What is your purpose?"

She had no answer. He knew it.

"Stop that ship," he said, to someone else. The other two ships turned toward the moon. "Mrs. August, we will board your ship and establish your identity. This will all be sorted shortly, I am sure."

The Reverend Mother sat down in the chair in front of the navigation array. She rested her hands on the soft nubs sticking up from the console, each one a nerve ending that, when touched, sent electrical impulses rushing through the ship's brain, directing it onward through space. She touched the one that activated the secondary chemical thrusters, and the ship shivered. These were for emergencies only. The auxiliary engines gave them a temporary burst of great speed, for just a few seconds, greater than anything the ship could accomplish under biological power. It would be enough speed to surprise the military cruisers. They would not be able to evade her.

～

"They're gaining," Jared said. He had bitten his thumb to the quick, and left a pinkish smear across the steel of the navigation console. "I think we'll be able to land, but they're coming up so fast, they'll be able to incinerate us before we can scatter." The ship lurched as it broke the atmosphere. Outside, the world was on fire. The heat of reentry. Gemma pressed against the porthole and she saw the dark shadow of the third military cruiser coming up hard behind them like a wolf who'd caught the scent of prey.

Jared banked hard, curving around above the colony to slow their speed. The cruiser stayed right on their tail. Below, the fields and homes of Terret's colony came into view, so small they looked like playthings yet.

"It's breaking off," Vauca whispered, pressed against the opposite porthole, like she didn't believe it. "It's breaking off."

It seemed unbelievable. Gemma held her breath until her chest hurt. But the cruiser stopped and turned and vanished back into the clouds.

Jared brought them around again and landed the ship in a field a dozen meters away from the colony's farmland. They did not see any of the soldiers yet, but one of the shuttles sat just across an empty field. Something felt very wrong. Gemma peered into the sky, but there was no sign of the cruiser. There was no explanation for it.

She might have thought it a miracle, but then Sister Lucia made a sound, a sound halfway between a gasp and a sob, like all the air was rushing out of her lungs at the point of a knife. Gemma looked and saw immediately what had happened. On the screen a white line showed the trajectory of the *Our Lady of Impossible Constellations*, the point where it was and the point where it had been. The line between the two cut straight through the military cruisers. She thought, absurdly, about the old maps of constellations and the imaginary lines drawn between one star and another. She couldn't think too hard about the rest—about how a collision like that would shred even a living ship's callused skin.

"Hush," Sister Faustina said, and laid a hand on Sister Lucia's shoulder, though not unkindly. "That won't keep them forever. Let's go before they remember us."

"She's dead."

"Very likely. Possibly not. Either way she wouldn't want you to hesitate."

That gathered them all up. Gemma could imagine the carnage above—bits of the cruisers turning to sparks and molten metal as they careened through the atmosphere, the *Our Lady of Impossible Constellations* bleeding out into the vacuum and the blood freezing to droplets of green ice, the Reverend Mother's skin turning gray and blue from lack of air. She could imagine it, but it would not be real until she saw it, so she put it out of her mind, strapped on her faceplate, and ran with the others for the colony.

They scattered as they reached the buildings. A rumble split the air and Gemma threw herself to the ground but it was only two of the shuttles taking off to go help their comrades stranded in the ships the Reverend Mother had disabled above. That left one. How many soldiers—four? Six? It didn't matter. They had lost so much time already. Her head was full of incubation periods and life expectancies. They stood on the narrow edge of hope.

She broke into the first home and found a body. A young man—younger than Lucia even, barely an adult—with pink foam still bursting at the edges of his lips. He was not long dead. She said a prayer for his soul and closed his eyes, but she could not give any more than that. If their treatment worked, and they stabilized the colonists, they would have to get off this moon as quickly as they could. There would be no washing and burying of the dead. They'd need to set fire to everything, if they even had time for that. She stopped for one bare second over the crest of a hill and looked down at what would have been a spinnery, what would have been the communal dining hall, what would have been the town square. So much hope bundled into these bricks and walls.

There was no wind today. Everything hung eerily still.

She would have given anything to hear even the clomping metal-soled boots of an ECG marine, but it did not come. She went to the meal hall and tried to open the door. Something was wrong with it. It hung askew in its track and refused to slide open. She threw her body against it—it moaned, and gave.

The air inside was stale and hot and hazy with mold spores. It stank of old blood and emptied bowels. She was glad for the face mask. Through the haze she saw two people slumped over a table. They were dead for certain—flies circled them, picking off bits of flesh. She stepped forward to search the rest of the building, and her foot collided with something metallic.

She looked down. A Central Governance soldier was sprawled at her feet. His stomach was torn open, gray coiled insides glistened wetly in the light from the open door. Now she could hear something, from the far end of the hall. Labored breathing.

So it was this advanced. She had thought she would be shaking, but she had never felt this sure in her life. She was meant for this. This was her duty. Either she would help this person or they would kill her, those were the options, and that was good and right.

She saw him cowered in the doorway, dark stains on his shirt. He heard her approaching and looked up, and even in the dark light she knew that he was blind. The pink and orange rings filled his eyes. One of his hands was bloody and mangled from tearing through the soldier's suit.

"Do you remember me?" she asked. His chest heaved, up and down, up and down. By now he had blood in his lungs. She did not know his name but she remembered his face at the wedding feast, smiling as he passed her rice and water. He'd had a nice smile, a shy one. Next to him lay the soldier's medical kit, scattered. Scalpels, vials, needles. What stupidity. Trying to threaten a ringeye victim who was still able to move.

She knelt next to him. He did not see her but he heard her and his hands convulsed in claws. She did not know of anyone who had survived this disease, but some of the scientists who had watched victims as they died said that it seemed the people were still locked inside their bodies, like they were resisting the aggression and the manic rage every moment. She had mixed a sedative into each dose of the treatment she had on hand. She just had to get it into him, and they would both be safe.

She touched his arm. He shuddered at the feel of her glove on bare skin. She readied a syringe and moved her hand slowly from his elbow to his shoulder to his collarbone, where she could tilt his chin back to get the needle in. His heartbeat quickened under her hand.

"Just a little longer," she said.

And then his eyes burst open and he jumped on her. She managed to hold onto the syringe but his knee went into her stomach and even through the vacsuit skin she felt something soft and vulnerable bruise. His hand went around her throat. She gasped. But she could feel the tension in him, his muscles contracted halfway between strangling her and letting her go, his mind fighting with the animal instincts taking over his body neuron by neuron. She pried her hand out from under herself and got the needle into the bulging vein in his neck. His ringed eyes drooped, and then he fell on top of her, silent and spent. She pulled herself up to sitting. His face was wet—she thought it was saliva and phlegm but when she looked, it was tears leaking from the corners of his eyes.

She sat with him in the ruins of his community for some long moments that she shouldn't have spared, smoothing his salt-flecked hair back from his forehead, until he was truly asleep.

~

Sister Lucia readied another syringe while Sister Faustina shouldered down the door to Terret and Joseph's home with three tries. These war-surplus prefabs had three rooms—a front room, a bedroom, and a bathroom. The front room looked like the family had just stepped out. A glass of water sat on a crate being used as a central table, a tablet lay in the chair. A blue crocheted blanket was folded neatly over the side of the crib.

They both went to the crib. The baby lay still inside.

"Oh, little one," Sister Faustina said, and crossed herself.

Babies were so dependent on calories. They burned so many trying to grow and starved so quickly. Poor, small soul. Sister Lucia reached in and rubbed the baby's still-pink cheek. And then—his small fingers reached for her hand. He didn't have the strength to cry but his eyes opened and focused on her. "Oh!"

She dropped her bag and fished out the formula they had brought. Just sweetened, fattened soymilk because they did not have real formula on board, but it was calories. She cradled him in the crook of her arm and wet his lips with the formula until he latched. Three mouthfuls, four, and she pulled the bottle away. She could kill him just as easy with too much at once. She had no idea how long he had been here, crying himself out with no one to answer.

"If the baby's here," Sister Faustina said, "Terret and Joseph must be too. They wouldn't have left him."

Sister Lucia swaddled the baby, let him have a last suck on the bottle, and put him back in the crib where he would be safe. Sister Faustina tried the doors to the bedroom and the bathroom; both were locked.

"Which one?"

Every hair on Sister Lucia's body was standing upright, her palms were sweating so the nitrile gloves stuck to her skin, she swore she could hear every sound in the village and every color looked like the truest version of itself. Adrenaline. Prey response. "The bedroom. More space."

Sister Faustina nodded. The locks on these interior doors were not so sturdy as the ones outside, and there was no reason to have electronic locks on a small, communal-property colony. She popped it easily with a knife from the kitchen. She paused before she opened it. "Did you notice? You can lock the bedroom from the outside. You can only lock the bathroom from the *inside*."

Sister Lucia didn't understand what she was getting at, but before she could ask, Sister Faustina swung open the door.

Joseph lunged at them, his eyes pink and orange with as many rings as a very old tree. He could not see them—Sister Lucia knew that even as she searched desperately for somewhere to hide if she needed it. He opened his mouth and licked at the air like he could taste the hot, stinking fear-sweat wetting under her arms. He was far gone enough for the rage to have taken over, but not far enough for his body to have started eating itself and his strength with it. His hands were bloody but she didn't know where the blood was coming from.

A hissing, gurgling sound came from his mouth. Sister Lucia thought it was just phlegm hacking up from his lungs but then he made it again and she realized he was begging them to stay away.

"Joseph, you must try to stay still," Sister Faustina said, like she was talking to a child getting ready for his vaccinations. Sister Lucia readied a dose of the treatment. "I know it is very difficult." His head turned, slowly, toward the sound of her voice. His legs trembled, readying to leap upon her. But she still had her sight and she jumped on him first, wrestling him to the ground and pulling his head back. "Lucia!"

Sister Lucia leapt down into the fray and held Joseph's flailing left arm down with her knee. Sister Faustina had his head but his teeth snapped dangerously close to her gloved hand. Animal whines burst from his throat. They were hurting him. The disease was taking its toll on his platelets—he was bruising already where they held him. Sister Faustina cupped her hands under his chin to stop him from wrenching his neck around but that left his other arm free to grab for Sister Lucia's face mask. She meant to be gentle; she could not be. She got the syringe through his skin in a way that left blood running down the hollow of his throat. He gargled on some loose fluid in his throat, and seized, and then finally lay still.

Sister Faustina went to wipe the sweat off her forehead and then realized she couldn't. She settled for leaning back against the wall instead. "Come on. Help me get him onto the couch."

Together they lifted him up and set him on his side in case he vomited. Sister Lucia lifted up his shirt and patted down his legs, looking for wounds. "I don't understand where this blood is from."

Sister Faustina pointed silently at the floor. Red streaks led under the bathroom door. Sister Lucia sucked in a breath so fast her lungs ached for it. Sister Faustina tapped the tip of her knife into the lock and jiggled it until it popped.

Terret lay curled in front of the washbasin, cradling the distress beacon. Dark brown blood, dried now, splattered the edge of the basin and the washtub and the composting toilet. Sister Lucia turned her over and found long, deep gouges across her shoulder and chest and belly, the kind made by ragged nails.

"She locked Joseph in the bedroom and herself in here," Sister Lucia whispered.

"And the baby in the front room where neither of them could hurt him." Sister Faustina crossed herself, which she so rarely had the urge to do.

Sister Lucia pressed her fingers under Terret's throat. She had a pulse. Weak, thready, irregular. She peeled open Terret's eyelids. She was infected, but only her irises were ringed with color, and not the whites. Still. Even if they cured her, she had been bleeding blood that wouldn't clot for days. Sister Lucia injected the antibodies into her system and then cut her shirt off to see how bad the damage was. Field stitching was not ideal, but she needed to get some of these wounds cleaned and closed.

Something clattered in the front room, like a cup dropping. Sister Lucia jumped, and Terret mumbled something desperate in her delirium.

"I thought you said there was sedative enough in there to drop a horse," Sister Faustina said. Her face mask was fogged with her own sweat. "I'll go."

~

Sister Faustina kept the little knife in her hand, even though she knew it would do nothing for her. She rounded the corner from the bathroom and saw Joseph's head still slumped on the arm of the couch. Not even his fingers twitched. Just the last flails of the disease before the sedative really took hold then? Or a seizure?

Click.

She turned, to the one corner of the room hidden from her. The ECG soldier pressed up against the wall pointed his rifle at her chest. His kit was on the floor by his feet. Two scalpels, specimen jars, empty syringes. What all were they taking from these people? No wonder so many dead soldiers lay in the square—the soldiers had put these people through pain, and the people in their delirium had fought back. She dropped the knife, and lifted her hands.

"I am not infected," she said. "I am a Sister of the Order of Saint Rita. I am here to offer aid."

He was really just a boy. A surplus child gathered up from an overcrowded planet and sent here, so far from home, to kill people whose names he would never know and be killed, eventually, by someone who would never remember his face. He held the rifle steady, but his eyes were wet. "Move away or I will kill you."

"If you take samples from that man, you will very well kill him. He's extremely sick. He's a good man, he doesn't deserve to die. And you know what your superiors are planning to do with this."

"He's a monster," he whispered. For the first time, she noticed the hairline crack running up the front of his faceplate, and the misting of blood on the front of his armor. "They are monsters. I saw—they killed my squadron. And you. You rammed your ship into my ship. My friends might be dead up there—"

She had no answer for that. In protecting them, the Reverend Mother had done something terrible to someone else. She had bought their safety with someone else's pain. It was not just or right but she had to believe it was the lesser evil. She stepped closer to the boy. She had never known how to soothe, so she did not try. "I took a vow of pacifism. I will not hurt you. But I will not let you hurt him, either."

She would never, for all the rest of her life, be able to explain what happened next. The air in the room changed and grew hot, like they were standing in front of the fire. The once-pale light through the open door filled the room with gold. She was seized, suddenly, by the idea that she could see inside this boy, see all his hopes and dreams and fears, and the small desire beating in his very deepest heart of hearts longing for *home home home*.

She unstuck her dry tongue from the roof of her mouth. She was filled with a great lightness. She did not understand but the current swept her along. "Please. My son. Don't you want to go home? There are different lives for you than this."

The light in the room faded as soon as it had come. The rifle barrel trembled and then he lost his hands and it fell. And he fell to his knees in the dried streaks of Terret's blood, on the floor of a home that was not his own, in the armor of a government that he knew now had turned him cruel and monstrous and sent him here to die and unleash death. Sister Faustina wrapped her arms around him and she felt hot tears on her own cheeks, for everything lost here.

~

In the end, if this had been a battle, they did not win. Of the original score-and-ten colonists, seven lived, including the baby. None of them could remember from their fever-dreams if the soldiers had taken any of their tissues, but it seemed likely, based on the number of bodies with rifle holes in them, that samples of the disease had left with the third ship and were currently jumping across the four system back to Earth where they would be weaponized. They had no soldiers to ask—the only live one left was the boy sobbing into Sister Faustina's arms, and he had not managed to take anything himself.

By the time the *Cheng I Sao* reached orbit again, the *Our Lady of Impossible Constellations* had bled out. Her armor plates were engaged still, the skin trying to heal itself around the navigation bay, loyal to the last. Inside they found the Reverend Mother's body. She had died with one hand around the emblem of St. Rita, and she had died smiling. The escape pod with Father Giovanni was nowhere to be found, and it was anyone's guess where he had gone.

Sister Lucia could never be all right with this—not

with any of it—but she hoped the old woman had found some measure of peace at the end. When they had wrapped her body in its shroud and let it out into space she had wanted to scream after it all of her questions and her anger. She had not been hurt, but she had lost something. An essential belief. She had felt it crack and slip away as soon as they saw their dead ship and she had known she would never be able to ask the Reverend Mother any of the questions eating their way through her guts.

"You've been very quiet," Gemma said. They'd limped their way to a station near the center of the system over the course of two weeks, dragging the corpse of the *Our Lady of Impossible Constellations.* At the station, there was too much work to be done, and none of them had felt like talking. There were supplies to be bought and survivors to care for and arrangements to make. Sister Lucia had not spoken to her old friend in days.

"Have you come to say goodbye?"

Gemma shrugged. "We're not leaving until tomorrow. I just wanted to talk to you."

And Sister Lucia had wanted desperately to talk to her, but now that they were together she had both far too much and far too little to say. She longed for those easy days of standing in the laboratory together, when it was just a fun puzzle and lives didn't hang in the balance.

When it seemed their whole small, anonymous lives would be spent traipsing across the system helping earthquake victims and writing hagiographies. But nothing remained of that life or that future.

"I don't know what to do," Lucia admitted.

"Well, from what Sister Faustina says, it's likely you'll be elected Mother Superior tomorrow."

"How am I supposed to lead anyone when—" Sister Lucia cut off. "I don't think I'll ever be sure of anything again, Gemma."

"The Reverend Mother was clearly no saint." Neither of them could bring themselves to call her Mrs. August, and that surely had not been her real name anyway. That was lost to history. "But she tried. And you are my dearest, oldest friend, and I know you have a good heart to guide you. There's much to be done, now. Especially without the Church's support."

They had taken the vote as soon as they docked at the station, and unanimously decided to declare themselves an independent order. Sister Ewostatewos sent the notice to the Church to make it official. Through a system of relays, of course, so it would not arrive until long after they had departed. And Sister Mary Catherine had left them, for she was shaken too deeply in her faith. Sister Lucia had not realized she would miss her, but she did.

"We can do small goods, but we can't take on Earth.

Not alone, and certainly not without abandoning our vows," Sister Lucia said. "I just keep thinking—is that enough?"

Gemma smiled and nodded across the station. "It was enough for them."

Sister Lucia looked across. Joseph and Terret and baby Keret sat in the mess hall, eating. Terret's cane leaned against her side. She had spent a long time without enough oxygen, and while her mind was intact, her right leg would not obey her. There would not be another chance at a new world for her. They would have to go somewhere with infrastructure to till the fields and build the homes for them. And they would have to change their names, all of them, because they would be hunted now. They would not be safe. But when Sister Lucia saw Terret lean down and press her nose into Keret's hair, she knew they would find it worth it.

"You're sure you're going to leave?" she asked.

Gemma nodded. "I think this life really is over for me. If anything would have changed my feelings—well. But I got you a new ship, didn't I?"

In the corpse of the *Our Lady of Impossible Constellations,* Gemma had found three larvae still clinging to life, developed enough to withstand the vacuum and warmed by the last heat from their dying siblings. The sisters had sealed the ship's flesh around them and hand-fed them protein slurry on the journey, and against all odds, they had survived. One shipling they had sold for their lodging and board and Gemma had taken the second, underdeveloped one for her menagerie. The third—Sister Lucia leaned against the porthole to see it. It had outgrown the lattice in the station's cargo bay and the shipwright on board had moved it out into space. It was growing nicely. Enough room, the shipwright had said, for a dozen women easy. It was glowing lightly green now, having received its first injection of symbiotic chloroplasts. Another month or two and it would be matured enough for them to christen it.

Vauca arrived with the supplies that Sister Lucia had asked her to beg, borrow, or steal for—growth medium and slides, vials and several strains of exotic antibiotics, testing strips. Everything she would need to perfect their treatment and hopefully, find a vaccine. Gemma leaned down to kiss Vauca, and they lingered on each other for just long enough that Sister Lucia knew she would never convince Gemma to return. She gathered the supplies up instead.

"Don't be a stranger."

"Of course not. It's not *that* big a system."

They both smiled, but they both knew it was the end of a great and glorious and innocent time. They knew what they could not forget; they had done what they could not undo. For now they could take a breath but very soon Central Governance would come calling, and the universe would change once more. There would be blood spilled again, across worlds and worlds, there might be war, or plague. And the universe would need them to do what small good things they could, even in the face of that which they could not stop. If all they could be were small rocks to break the current, it would have to be enough.

"Goodbye," Sister Lucia said, not just to Gemma but to that time when she had believed unquestioningly and loved so foolishly and freely. It hurt like a wound being stitched together, a necessary hurt, a hurt that would leave scar tissue but leave her healed. "Goodbye."

Outside, the stars glittered cold and uncaring, for they had endured long before humanity and would endure long after. She took comfort in them, and their light, as it reached to her through time. Some of those stars were gone, and they would not know for years; others had swelled to gas giants or collapsed to brown dwarfs, and yet the light that reached here was young and hale. She was one small part of an infinity, and there was much to be done.

Acknowledgments

No book (even a very short one) is possible alone. I owe all the thanks to the following: Jenna and Jesse Barnes, for their endless patience with my science questions; Cait Kostuck, for her cheerleading and kicks-in-the-pants in equal measure; Lexi Campell, Katie Jimenez-Gray, Matt McAloon, Matt Weaver, and Wes Wootten, for being very understanding about having a coworker who wanders around muttering about slugs; Aimee Ogden, for beta-reading the first version of this story and her smart critique; Dan Stout and Stephanie Lorée, for listening to my description of an oddball, too-long short story and saying "Maybe it's a novella?"; Mary Catherine Moeller, Michael Fealey, and Jaya Minhas, for being all-around good friends; and the SFF and writing communities who have been so kind and welcoming to a new writer. This book also would not have happened without the work of the Tor.com Publishing team, including Ruoxi Chen, Caroline Perny, Mordicai Knode, Amanda Melfi, Christine Foltzer, Drive Communications, and of course, editor extraordinaire Christie Yant. Thank you all for this weird and wonderful journey.

About the Author

Courtesy of the author

Lina Rather is a speculative fiction author from Michigan, now living in Washington, D.C. Her stories have appeared in a variety of publications, including *Shimmer, Flash Fiction Online,* and *Lightspeed.* When she isn't writing, she likes to cook, go hiking, and collect terrible '90s comic books.

TOR · COM

Science fiction. Fantasy. The universe.

And related subjects.

*

More than just a publisher's website, *Tor.com*
is a venue for **original fiction, comics,** and
discussion of the entire field of SF and fantasy,
in all media and from all sources. Visit our site
today—and join the conversation yourself.

CPSIA information can be obtained
at www.ICGtesting.com
Printed in the USA
LVHW101034080723
751745LV00004B/477

9 781250 260253